Pendragon

and

Merlin's Tomb

C.J. Brown

Pendragon Legend
Book One

Copyright © 2021 by C.J. Brown.

All rights reserved. No part of this book may be used or reproduced in any manner whatsoever without written permission except in the case of brief quotations embodied in critical articles or reviews.

This book is a work of fiction. Names, characters, businesses, organizations, places, events and incidents either are the product of the author's imagination or are used fictitiously. Any resemblance to actual persons, living or dead, events, or locales is entirely coincidental.

CONTENTS

1. Battle Royale 1
2. Barbarians at the Gate 7
3. Five Dragons 13
4. Preparing for Battle 19
5. Lookout Ridge 25
6. Palatine Hill 35
7. Krampus Rerouted 43
8. Cowardice in the Flesh 47
9. Interrogation 53
10. News From Rome 61
11. Attila the Hun 67
12. Into the City 75
13. Bishkar's Rise 87
14. Black Moon Rising 91

15. Peeling 97

16. Valley of Death 103

17. Vanished 111

18. The Enchanted Forest 115

19. Voyage 127

Newsletter 131

About the Author 133

*For my parents, who always
encouraged my creativity*

1

BATTLE ROYALE

WITH BALLS OF FIRE RAINING down on his troops, Arthur galloped to the front of the line. His cavalry on the left flank was now all but decimated. The one on his right, in the distance, was being routed. In moments, his men would be outflanked and the crushing blow to the tenth cohort of foot soldiers on the left would be complete. The men in the first cohort on his farthest right would soon be slaughtered by the sword-wielding cavalry of the enemy. With the flanks destroyed, Arthur knew that it would spell the end of the campaign.

Arthur was greeted upon reaching the front line with a spear that found its way into the chest of his mighty horse. With a loud cry, Boadicea, Arthur's trusted stallion, collapsed as his front legs buckled in pain. With no time to mourn his friend, Arthur leaped. Sword raised in flight, he descended on his quarry like the fist of God. With a swift blow, Arthur split the head of the soldier who had the misfortune of being in front of him. The metal of the helmet and the bone of his skull were no match against the steel of Arthur's sword.

Each body he slayed, every foot he pushed forward, allowed his army to weaken the front lines of the enemy. The cavalry was already lost. If they could just hold and protect the main mass of men, then they could penetrate the heart of the enemy and win the day. There was still a way to win this—the hardest battle of his young life.

Or so he thought.

As hope began to fill his heart and power his arms, a spear, launched from a catapult, found the blood-stained armor that protected his chest. As the tip of the spear ripped the metal of the armor, the crashing sound of iron on iron silenced the rest of the battle as Arthur watched, in apparent slow motion, and felt it bury itself into his chest. The sudden searing pain exploding from the point of impact rushed to his mind and jolted him out of a deep slumber, soaked in sweat.

Sitting in his bed, he watched as the fire in the hearth across from him burned brightly. As heir to the house of Pendragon, Arthur had the right to the largest chamber in the garrison's northern tower, but he chose more humble lodgings, amidst the men he fought with. His only luxury was this large fire now burning a few feet from him.

Arthur peered down at his chest that glistened with sweat. A sense of relief washed over him as he realized that the spear was part of a dream. In the neighboring quarters, the neighing of his horse—that distinctive snort of a thoroughbred, comforted him once more. It had indeed been a dream.

His muscles, still tight from the tense experience, took a moment to relax as he lowered his head into his hands. It might not have been real, and he was still alive, but the dream itself happened, and that was not a good omen. Pulling his tunic from the foot of his bed, he slipped into it and got out from between the thick layers of fur that kept him warm on the cold winter nights of northern Italy.

His caligae lay beside his bed, worn from heavy use, but still sturdy. They had thick soles and heavy leather straps that crisscrossed their way up to his knees. He strapped them on and stood up, moving to his heavy wooden stand where the rest of his ensemble hung. Donning his armor, he looked around the room for his cloak. His eyes caught sight of it on the chair behind his table. Papers on the table lay strewn across, covering every inch of the wood beneath it. Drawings and notes of the fortress's current expansion littered his table.

He glanced at them. The next morning, he would continue to oversee the extension of the southern wall. His father planned on raising a third legion in the northeast, after the expansion of his first legion, Gaul Fortis, in Genua. Genua was a much better place to be, Arthur thought. It sat nestled in a cove off the Mediterranean Sea and had a more suitable climate. Here, in Verona, on the other hand, which sat at the foothills of the Alps, it was drastically different. Still, he thought, consoling himself, it was better than being further north where his father planned a fourth legion.

Arthur snapped out of his thoughts about the work the next day and returned to the omen he had just viscerally experienced. There was something about the dream that was unnerving. Igraine, his mother, had always told him about the intangible forces that played in the background. She taught him about omens and spirits and how they were a part of a world that was greater than just wealth and conquest.

Fully dressed, he marched out of his quarters. The early dawn air was cold and damp. Somewhere in the distance, it rained. While unusual for this time of the year, showers were not unheard of. From where he stood, he couldn't see the men who were supposed to be on the garrison walls, nor the ones in the towers that marked the four corners of the structure. None of the soldiers on watch seemed to be patrolling the ramparts they were assigned to. It was desolate and deserted. Instead, the men were asleep.

Battles had not been fought at the garrison or in Verona, nearby, for more than a few years. As Rome's influence fell, fewer altercations on the border erupted.

MERLIN'S TOMB

There were lesser wars being fought as the emperor was not intent on conquering, but on defending his illegitimate throne.

Taking a deep breath and releasing a sigh at the lack of discipline in the early morning guards, Arthur made his way to the stone steps of the first tower on the southwest corner of the wall. He found men asleep at their posts all along the route that he used to ascend the top of the wall. There here found more men in blissful slumber.

With no fires blazing nearby, his eyes acclimated to the night sky. The cold wind from the north brushed past his face and swept his hair as it moved south, chilling the lands below it. In the distance, the white peaks of the Alps hid, obscured by the dark clouds of the impending storm.

He found the captain of the night watch sleeping at his station, on par with the men under his command.

"Captain!" Arthur boomed, shaking the man out of his slumber and causing him to nearly fall off his chair.

"My lord," he stuttered, half asleep, and half ashamed.

"Does this happen every night?"

The captain could not add to his shame by lying. "Yes, my lord. I am sorry. It just gets so quiet and boring and the men just fall asleep inadvertently."

"Well, it's not entirely their fault."

"No, my lord, it is mine."

"That's not what I meant, Captain. The men have had nothing to do for years and so there has been no urgency for discipline."

"Yes, my lord."

"But that's about to change, Captain," Arthur whispered, as he pointed to the slopes of the northeastern sky.

Urgency displaced the effects of early morning slumber as adrenaline pushed all measure of complacency out of him. As lightning struck, illuminating the lands, an invasion party lining the ridges made itself known.

"Keep things quiet. Do not blow the horn or beat the drums. We shall prepare in silence."

"Yes, my lord," the captain replied, quickly getting on his feet and making his way to the soldiers' quarters.

Arthur stood on the parapets, using each flash of lightning to gather intelligence of the army that lined the horizon. The best he could guess was that there were a thousand men who lined the periphery of vision. He calculated that to be about ten thousand men in total. The number that lay behind the ridge would not be visible and thus it was a good guess that there were ten thousand, double of what he had to command amongst the men who slept quietly.

"They will attack at dawn," he whispered to himself, concluding correctly that the tribes of Germania always waited for sunlight to attack. Checking the clepsydra—the water clock at the night station—he calculated that dawn was an hour away. The garrison usually needed three hours to deploy, but that was when they were fully awake. Now they would need more.

2

BARBARIANS AT THE GATE

THE BARBARIAN ARMY ARRIVED JUST before dawn. Gradually, they amassed under the cover of darkness until the full might of twenty thousand men lined the ridge of the northern slopes. In the valley below, a silent town lay before them. A decidedly ominous day would unfold as soon as the sun found its way past the horizon if the Huns were not stopped.

Twenty thousand men, draped in thick fur coats and clad in heavy iron armor, brandished their weapons with ease and extreme prejudice. Ahead of them, stood the first wave—the expendables, men not worth the mud they stood on. They were no more than slaves, tasked with absorbing the brunt of the opposing army on the field of battle. Their only purpose was to slow the opposing army by dying.

Amongst this group of expendables was a mismatch of ability and appearance. Some were short and stocky, others were thin and lanky. Farmers and bakers in another life, they stood shoulder to shoulder scared for what lay ahead but even more so of what lay behind.

They stood there, women and children amidst their ranks, against their will, and assembled as prisoners from villages the army had sacked. They were the second tier, dressed in a hodge-podge of attire. Some were not lucky enough to have warm clothing, others were even worse without any semblance of armor. The ones who did possess heavy iron to protect vulnerable flesh were considered fortunate. Among them, some wielded swords, others carried spears, harvested and sacked from their defeated enemies along a trail of destruction that spanned for their native land in the north.

This dual-layered attack posture had been successful over the last thousand miles and a dozen years. Every village they sacked provided them with food for the men, and more men for their front lines. The king got to keep the gold they sacked, while soldiers got to keep everything else, including the women of the village.

Behind them, they left a wake of destruction, marked by smoke from the smoldering ashes, broken bones of men who dared resist, and the shrieks of the old who were left amidst the devastation. The barbarian horde was ruthless in many respects, and the path they had carved through the countryside was evidence of that.

The clear skies of moments ago quickly filled with rain clouds, and quicker still, began to threaten a wet morning. With banners streaming in the wind, drenched in rain that now poured in droves, the silhouettes of a fearsome invading horde began to appear as the lightning flashed in rapid succession. As thunder clapped and the winds howled, sheets of torrential rain lashed the countryside, turning the meadows of summer into a pit of black mush.

Between the ridge where they stood and the pit of mush below, the rough terrain of northern Italy unfolded before them, flashing into view each time the lighting from the gods struck the ground and lit the scene. It was more apparent now than it had ever been for Adolphus, supreme general of the invading horde, that this was not a battle to be undertaken.

Something about the calm in the valley disturbed him.

Wet and cold, the heavens had chosen to make this campaign a difficult one, Adolphus believed. A superstitious man, he would always seek the security of rituals and the direction of omens in addition to the intelligence reports his riders brought back. This was much to his king's fury, as the latter was not a superstitious man. But still, the king gave him the room he needed. After all, Adolphus was undefeated. His strategies were sound, his execution, perfect.

As the barbarian army marched toward their quarry, they had done so with singular focus. The hundreds of cities they sacked and plundered along the way were designed for one purpose alone—to bulk up the army that would eventually reach the gates of Rome, the capital of the largest empire the world had ever seen.

Now only a fortnight's ride from the outer gates of the Roman capital, Adolphus began to focus on every aspect, and worry about every detail. The Huns had never ventured this far south, and even though Adolphus had navigated this campaign with a deft hand, the true test of the campaign was imminent. From the rear, his king would arrive in three days.

Ahead, the Roman legions loyal to Uther Pendragon sat beyond the town. There was only one thing in the world he was more afraid of than the fury of his own king, and it was the mind of Arthur.

Towering at seven feet tall, Arthur Pendragon was a giant once he mounted his Berber horse. Clasped in his armor, the sight of him stoked fear in the hearts of anyone who saw him lead the charge in battle. Never to be the one to stand on the hill, detached from the battle, Pendragon always fought with his men, and that earned him the loyalty and respect of every legionnaire across the provinces of the empire.

A nagging thought festered in the depths of his subconscious. Hardened in military campaigns for his entire adult life, and at the hilt of a sword since the age of eight, Adolphus could not shake the instinct that forewarned a problem. The Romans could not be so daft, he thought. This new emperor, he knew, lived high on the success of men who had gone before him. He was not the greatest of generals in battle, even though he was a schemer. But even he could not have been so foolish to not know that an army of twenty thousand barbarians was descending upon him.

Silence in the village below and darkness in the garrison beyond only meant they had succeeded in their clandestine intent. Or it could be that a trap was being set. Adolphus had to figure out which. If it was the latter, Adolphus had to figure out what that trap was and foil it. But he also knew that with his king only three days from arriving, he only had free reign for a limited time. The arrival of his king also meant the arrival of another ten thousand men. Thirty thousand battle-hardened soldiers bursting through the gates of Rome would put Emperor Lucius on his back heels. Once Rome fell, the rest of the empire would follow suit.

C.J. BROWN

3

FIVE DRAGONS

THE MORNING HOURS, SQUEEZED between the revelry of the night prior and the business of governing an empire the next morning presented an uncharacteristic silence as Rome slept. The scheming of the Senate, the debauchery of the bathhouses, and the treachery of the Imperial Palace had all taken the respite they desperately needed.

In the distance, under the shadow of the mighty Colosseum, a true Roman sat in his seat, his eyes fixed on the horizon where flames lit the perimeter of the Imperial Palace. In the light of day, Palatine Hill represented a sore reminder of events that changed the course of his family's history.

"This must not stand," he whispered, with his wife standing beyond earshot.

The canter of a fast-approaching Berber echoed clearly in the distance against that backdrop of pre-activity silence, prompting a swift alteration of his countenance.

"The rider approaches," he began, indicating that his wife now execute the plan they had devised in anticipation of his arrival.

A look of determination and fear mingled across the gentle features of Ingraine's countenance.

"I will be ready by the time he arrives," she said, moving with a little more haste in her preparations than a few moments earlier.

For his part, Uther, the patriarch of the family and the rightful heir to the throne, alighted from his chair and donned his breastplate. His coat of arms, emblazoned with five dragons coiled around the noble bay leaf wreath, signified the proud house of the five dragons.

Under that, his ceremonial lorica segmentata had already been in place since he prepared for the events that were about to unfold. The segmentata, consisting of the steel body armor that wrapped around the seven-foot man's torso, had never seen the blood of battle. His attire this morning was purely ceremonial. It was what he wore when in the audience of Emperor Lucius.

Each segment of the armor had been polished to a high shine. Not a single scratch tarnished it. Not a single smudge robbed it of its luster. In the light of the fire that burned fiercely in the hearth of the dining room, Uther Pendragon sent shimmering light to all corners of his palatial home. His tunic beneath the armor was a bright crimson, made from the best wool Italy could procure. Not a single stitch was out of place and it fit his frame like a glove.

The breastplate was uncommon among the soldier class and seen on most generals. But Uther was not the same as those men. He was the tip of the spear, the patriarch of a long line of emperors. His father, Constantine III, was the founder of the House of Pendragon and grandson to Emperor Constantine, the protector of the Roman Catholic Church.

The galea that sat on the table, with the plume made of fine horse hair and dyed bright red, was to accompany him on this trip. Placing it over his bald head, he let the solid copper helmet slide down his round head, giving him the protection it deserved while bestowing upon him the power of his standing.

With his pteruges in place and his greaves snugly fitted, Uther Pendragon walked out his front door to meet his horse and the rider who was approaching. With a swift leap, he mounted Bucharia, his steed, and adjusted the seat of his saddle, biding his time for the rider who approached. When he did arrive, the two men nodded. A polite greeting was exchanged in silence between two men who had immense respect for one another.

The older of the two, Uther saw the younger as someone who embodied the honor now missing from the typical Roman. The younger one saw a wise teacher in the elder.

"Keep her safe," he whispered, so as to not allow his words to fall on his wife's ears.

"I will, my lord."

A nod followed, indicating approval.

"What news from Arthur?"

"He complains about the cold that is descending from the Alps, but the job on the fortress proceeds apace."

Uther nodded, knowing full well that his son did not like the climate, but all the more reason, if that be the case, Uther thought, that he needed to remain where he was.

Uther was a clever tactician. He raised armies and placed them where they were needed. The first one was a deterrent to the Gallic armies in the northwest. The second was a deterrent to the Germanic tribes in the northeast. These two garrisons were the reason behind the peace that had descended onto Rome and made the emperor fat.

In Verona, two legions would eventually fortify the Limes Germanicus—the border between the Roman Empire in the south of Germania and the tribes in the north. When it was all done, Arthur was to command both legions on his father's behalf.

The current legion that Arthur commanded, Gemina Maxima, when supplemented, would be a companion legion of Gemina Minima. Ten thousand strong, they would be a formidable force in the northeast and keep any aspirations of the barbarian tribes in check. Uther had designed the defensive mechanisms to require the might of two legions. He did so specifically to overcome the consequences of the erroneous decisions that Emperor Lucius was making when he pulled soldiers back from the frontier to augment the barricades around the city and the Imperial Palace.

C.J. BROWN

4

PREPARING FOR BATTLE

THE CITY AT THE FOOT of the hills, impervious to the intruders atop, was one steeped in history. Sitting on the front lines of the Western Roman Empire, it was the backbone of the strategic outpost, designed not just to protect, but to be a launching platform for aspirations in the far east. It rose from the mud to support the forward garrison and grew to prominence during the heyday of the empire.

On the ridge, Adolphus evaluated his plan in silence. His heart was set on a plan, but something tugged at him.

"Will they yield, my lord?" Bassich, the six-foot lieutenant asked.

"I hope they don't. The men need a victory on the eve

of our greatest battle yet. And the best victory comes from a full-hearted battle, not from the opponent's surrender," Adolphus answered.

"Indeed. The men have been looking forward to this battle but there isn't a lot to plunder here."

"Send word to the captains. We strike the city at dawn," Adolphus commanded.

"Yes, my lord," Bassich replied as he bowed. Pulling on the reins, the lieutenant peeled his horse from where it stood and rode off to do his General's bidding. To take his place by the General's side, another lieutenant, Hinkin of Gaul, strode up to the line on his horse.

"My lord," Hinkin began, "we are ready upon your command."

"Are we certain," Adolphus asked, "that the garrison beyond is not a problem?"

"According to our spies, the men have grown fat, the garrison is being worked on, and even now they are asleep. No fire and no activity. Our spies who rode by the wall heard only the sounds of slumber," Hinkin answered.

"Very well. How far distant to the walls of the garrison?"

"Five leagues to the northern wall, my lord," the man from Gaul with a good gauge of the land, responded.

"That puts them out of range of the trebuchets," Adolphus advised, realizing that it was positioned there for that reason.

"Yes my lord, the trebuchets behind the ridge will hit

the town precisely where we want them to, but they will not be able to come anywhere near the garrison."

"We shall not waste our time with them. Focus on the town. It will be over by noon."

The men had already begun constructing the catapults and the siege engines. It would be ready by daybreak. Adolphus, still sitting atop his steed, trotted off the ridge, heading back behind it to inspect the men and the equipment. Much of the equipment, now drenched in rain, was covered in mud and blood. The men were tired, he realized. A day's delay in the attack would be a better option.

Adolphus looked back as if to seek direction from the omens of the valley but the ridge had shielded his view and he could not see the fortress any longer. Even if they were a skeletal crew, he thought, they would still send scouts, and those scouts may stumble upon this camp. The element of surprise would be lost if they waited one more day.

"No," he said resolutely. "We attack at dawn," he whispered to himself.

Dawn arrived in due course and the forward army of prisoners suited up. With fear on their faces and pain in their hearts, they bowed to their gods and asked for mercy and good fortune to not be slayed by the blades of the enemy.

***

The commander of the expendable army, a Hun, mounted

his horse with ferocity, yelling at the top of his lungs. Commanding his captains, positioned at ten-pace intervals all along the left and right of him, he directed them to begin the attack.

The commander and his captains led from the rear, pushing the expendables down the ridge. Chasing them for the express purpose of gaining momentum and barreling down into the town below, he was merciless in his endeavor. Anyone who fell on the rocky slopes was trampled over while the rest were pushed harder until they reached the bottom of the hill and began their charge on the fields and the town. Farmers and citizens watched the thundering expendables in horror.

Watching the scene unfold, Adolphus sat still on his horse high on the ridge. Six flagmen accompanied him. His opening gambit was proceeding as planned, he thought, as he turned to look at the town below. Still, there was no defense being mounted by the town or the men from the garrison beyond. A smile came over his face.

Behind the ridge, ten thousand men waited for the command to attack. Their commander sat mounted on his steed, looking to the ridge where Adolphus and the six flagmen sat perched. The commander was battle-hardened, towering above six feet tall, with a red beard down to his belly, braided in two, side by side. His red hair, indicative of his ancestry, was long and tied into a Suebian knot. The troops called him Krampus, the personification of evil. He wore no armor. Only iron greaves protected his legs.

To shield against the cold, he wrapped himself with bison fur. Even in the harshest of winters and in the most bitter of battles, that was all he wore. To show for his lack of armor, he had a dented skull and a crooked arm—fused in place when a broken bone set without being straightened. He had numerous gashes across his back, injuries that healed then became injured again until they looked like fish scales.

Krampus took to killing men like fish to water. His first kill was at the age of nine, though some say, he had killed his father when he turned seven. Even Adolphus never warmed up to him, but he knew Krampus to be the best means to keep the expendables in check and to provide the example needed to kill whatever lay in front of him.

Adolphus turned to his flagmen and signaled his intentions. Instantly, the flags went up to communicate those intentions to the rest of the forces. This time it was to ready the fireballs, loaded and locked in the trebuchets. Seeing from his perch that the fires had been lit and all the balls of the first line were ready, he issued the next command. This was quickly translated and the appropriate flags quickly rose for all to see. With this command, the arms were released, sending balls of fiery tar high into the air. They had been calibrated to strike just beyond the town.

C.J. BROWN

5

LOOKOUT RIDGE

"**G**ENERAL, THE FIRST GROUP OF men are ready. We will mobilize on your command," Vipsanius, the Captain of Arthur's army, announced. They had assembled behind the walls of the fort in record time.

"Move Delphi Company through the northern forest, take the pass to reach behind the ridge, and wait till I arrive on the other side," Arthur instructed his man.

"Behind the ridge, my lord?" The Captain furrowed his brows, perplexed that they were not about to attack the invaders head-on.

"Yes, Captain Delphi Company is to go by foot. No horses. And do so in absolute silence. The forest is still dark and you will not be seen. Let the fires in the garrison extinguish naturally. Do not relight them or douse them. Understand?"

"Yes, my lord." The captain obeyed. He suddenly came to realize Arthur's intentions.

"You lead Delphi Company on that objective. Leave Romulus Company in the basement of the garrison. I will lead Remus Company through the southern forest and around the other side. We will flank them," Arthur confirmed.

Upon receiving his detailed instructions, Captain Vipsanius nodded, saluted his general, and hurried away to make it so. Within the hour, ahead of schedule and prior to the arrival of the first sliver of light, both companies vacated the garrison, invisible to the spies on the ridge.

Arthur and his company of men had a greater distance to cover but had horses to make up the time. Two thousand well-trained legionaries, a little fat in the belly perhaps, but as effective as can be, moved with resolve toward the western pass.

This section of the range stretched from northeast to southwest mountain range that sloped down toward Verona. The forests on either side and the town of Verona in the clearing were as picturesque as any hamlet south of the Alps.

The southern pass Arthur and his company were headed for was not a commonly known passage through the range. Most foreigners rose to the top of the ridge and descended down the leeward side, just as Adolphus had done. The pass was a clandestine path the legions used to move in and out of the plains. It was tricky enough for untrained horses that even if the northerners knew about it, they chose not to take the path. It usually whittled down the number of horses they had and slowed them down a great deal.

For Arthur and his men, they knew the pass like the back of their hand, giving them a tremendous advantage. As they passed the forest, within sight of the pass, they witnessed fireballs streak across the sky destined for the town.

They couldn't reach the garrison, so why aim there? Arthur thought, as he navigated his horse and rode it hard. Soon he realized that the invaders were building a line of fire to cut the men from the garrison off from coming to the aid of the town.

There was no time to waste and he had to think on his feet. The battle with an enemy that relied on brute force could only be won with strategy, he decided.

As the foot soldiers under Vipsanius raced amidst the dense and dark forest of the northern Italian landscape, Arthur's cavalry and archers moved swiftly, weaving between the trees until they arrived at the pass. Without hesitation, they began their ascent up the sharp edges of the pass and the uneven gradient of the slope. The darkness would have been a problem if it were not for the practice they had in navigating the spot. The path was a mere three cubits wide and spelled certain doom for the uninitiated.

The further he galloped, the more his eyes acclimated to the darkness increasing his odds for success. The harder he rode, the more adept he became with the path and his horse. The two now moved as one—a centaur with the mind of a man and the speed of a horse. As he made his way around the bends and avoided the potholes, he found himself at his destination—the forest southwest of the open field that the Huns had staked out. Here, he stopped. If his calculations were right, Vipsanius should have arrived on the northeast side of the clearing directly opposite Arthur, with the Huns, unwittingly, in between.

The clearing in the center housed the camps and, ahead of them, the men in attack formation, ready to crest the ridge and follow the expendables. Arthur looked carefully. Until now he hadn't laid eyes on any of them. But now, as the sun began to spread a shimmer of light, he could recognize the banners.

"Huns," he said, exasperated at the revelation. This is too far south for them to have ventured. Of all the tribes in Germania, the Huns were the most feared. But fear was not what crossed his mind at this point. It was revulsion. He now had a good idea of what the men would do to the townspeople. The desire to save the people remained at the top of his mind. But Arthur knew that by doing so it would cripple the entire endeavor. The Hun army was vicious. In a battle of equal number, the Romans would lose five men for every barbarian they lost.

Arthur had no choice. To win this battle, the townsfolk would have to be bait for now. That would be better for Rome. As he pondered the calculus of war and politics, the rear guard of the troop arrived to brief him on the status of the company.

"We only lost twenty-five men and horses in the pass."

"Understood."

"Who are these men, General?" he asked.

"Huns," Arthur replied in disgust.

"This far south?"

"It would seem."

"The town, my lord. Are we going to do anything about the town?"

Arthur shook his head. He had already had this conversation with himself and the answer was going to be no different.

"But my lord," the captain insisted. "We have a duty to protect them."

"What's your name and rank, soldier?"

"Linus Marcellus, captain of the Eighth Cohort."

"Captain Linus, you will hold your tongue or I will relieve you of it. You have sat fat at the garrison for so long that you do not know your place."

"My lord, I am merely pointing out the moral choices here."

"Moral choices? Are you a soldier or a philosopher? In

the field of battle, at this stage, there are no moral choices. Here, there are only choices of life and death and I will be judged not by the sanctity of my choices or how moral they may be but by the numbers who live and die today and to protect Rome."

"Forgive me, my lord. What would you have me do?'

"We proceed as planned."

"Yes, my lord."

Arthur surveyed the scene. There were at least ten thousand men encamped in the valley, not in battle mode. Just before the ridge, getting ready to cross over and join the attack were another ten thousand men. He could see Adolphus high on the ridge with his six flagmen.

Calling his lieutenant, he instructed him on what needed to happen next. There was a slight change in plans, but not by much.

"As soon as I give you the sign, alert Vipsanius and begin the attack. These men are not expecting an attack and those men will not be able to turn back once they accelerate down the hill."

"Understood, my lord.

Arthur evaluated his next move and plotted his course to his objective. The commander in the center had begun to prepare to launch the wave of men behind the expendables. There was a point in the operation that he knew would present the best opportunity. He knew what he had to do.

Arthur repositioned his horse and pointed it at

Adolphus, then began galloping up the hill under the cover of the trees. No one except his men, now hidden by the tree line, could see him. His gallop was swift, his resolve, steel.

As he approached, Adolphus had given the order for the second wave to follow the expendables. In the same moment, Arthur had galloped clear of the forest cover and was now in the open. As the last man of the Hun army made it over the ridge and began accelerating down the slopes, Arthur charged Adolphus.

Arthur, clad in his battle armor, from helmet to greaves, with his red cloak flying in his wake, presented a fearsome turn of events. Young, and in his prime, he was not just a sharp general but an able swordsman and an expert at hand to hand combat.

Perched on the lookout point on the ridge, Adolphus had not expected to be ambushed by a charging Roman. There was no sign the flagmen could conjure to tell the armies below that Adolphus himself was in peril. The bulk of the Hun forces now faced their backs to him and were already fully vested in the charge on the town below. Even if they could hear the horn to retreat—which they couldn't—momentum was against them.

Adolphus had not seen the Roman charging until his own horse neighed and became distracted by Arthur's approach. Much to Adolphus's surprise, he saw a Roman in full battle uniform riding hard toward him, not ten paces. Before he could react, Arthur was upon him. His flagmen were frozen in place by what they were witnessing. But Arthur had not given them time to consider their options. He leaped from his saddle with Boadicea galloping at full speed and was already landing on Adolphus before the six flagmen could move to prevent the situation.

The only eyes that were looking at the melee on the ridge were the men behind the treeline under Vipsanius' command. Silently, they cheered for their general, as they witnessed his ferocious charge upon the enemy. Leaping from his lightning-fast steed, he took to the air and, for a brief moment, his red cape and shining armor catching the light of the newborn sun, Arthur looked like a god in flight. They could almost see the look of fear descend on Adolphus's face as Arthur slammed into him and the two men tumbled to the ground.

If only they could cheer, the ground would have thundered in reverberation. Still, they kept an eye on the ignorant masses before them—the army that was not deployed in the day's campaign. The Huns remained focused on setting up their camp and preparing for the next campaign where they would be the hammer that fell on unsuspecting villagers.

The line of trebuchets had halted the launch of fireballs. Their job was to set the forest in the southeast ablaze, which they had accomplished perfectly. The forest between the town and the garrison now burned, spewing amber into the air as barks erupted and twigs raged. The tar flame that spread across the forest spread rapidly and made escaping from the city impossible. If the men from the fortress had tried to help, they would have been caught in the inferno that ensued. Arthur had decidedly wisely.

The flagmen had already conveyed the command to cease the launches, and the men operating the catapults now returned to camp so that the men in the garrison could not come to the villagers' aid.

Up on the ridge where Arthur battled the Hun general, the flagmen watched in shock as their commander struggled with the Roman, they did not see the six archers on horseback that had tailed Arthur. By the time the flagmen could react to Arthur's presence, six arrows found their way through their backs. One by one they fell, leaving Adolphus to face the youthful power of General Arthur Pendragon.

Getting up off the mud, with the rain still pouring on his face, Arthur surveyed the land for his sword. It was farther than he had hoped it would be, and reaching for it might be a tactical error. On his left, the Hun general was moving toward his blade and would reach it in less time than it would take Arthur to get to where he needed to be. Instead of relying on metal, Arthur decided to rely on muscle and sinew. Once again, Arthur launched and landed on the general who was beginning to regain his wits, clarity, and balance. This time the pounce was effective as he landed on the barbarian's back.

Placing his arm around the man's neck, Arthur gripped it tightly, causing Adolphus to struggle. But the struggle was futile. The Roman's grip was beyond reproach. The struggle between the two men continued, both still full of energy. Both unwilling to yield. But in time, the weight of the Roman began to overpower the Hun. And, coupled with the pressure on his neck, Adolphus began to suffocate.

Rather than the lack of energy required to do battle, it was the weight of a full-grown man and his armor that vanquished the older general. As his sight began to fade, he struggled even more. Arthur hung on tirelessly, tightening his grip around the man's neck. His goal was to let the life of the older general slip into the underworld.

6

PALATINE HILL

THE MARBLE PILLARS OF THE Imperial Palace stretched skyward, capped by an intricately ornate roof. Artistry adorned the roofs to symbolize the heavens and the sanctity of the emperor's rule over the land. Ever since Augustus Caesar, every emperor for five hundred years had claimed that they were the son of the divine and the carvings in the ceiling and pillars attempted to symbolize that.

The marble that was used in each of those pillars had come from quarries in Italy and the furthest extent of the provinces. No expense had been spared over time to upgrade the palace. Only one other palace existed, and that was Emperor Nero's. Nero's palace had been buried in mud after he committed suicide. All that was left now to symbolize the might of the empire was the Imperial Palace.

"Why is he here?" the emperor demanded. A stocky man with a receding hairline, Emperor Lucius believed himself to be valiant and brave, but as far from it. His arms were filled with flab where men of better mettle stored muscle.

"He says that he has news of the northern garrisons and wishes to seek your approval to proceed with the expansion," Titus, the emperor's aid, answered.

"It is not the emperor's job to maintain his garrison. Is this a threat on his part?"

"I am not certain as to his objectives. I am only guessing what they could be. But if you ask me, I would not trust him. After all, I am certain that he is still desirous of your throne. If he had usurped it from you, wouldn't you be desirous of the throne, sire?"

Emperor Lucius was incensed at the response. But it made sense. Of course, Lucius would be upset if such a situation happened to him, and find every way possible to grab the throne from the usurper.

"Is that what he's here to do?" Lucius whispered aloud, asking himself.

"I—"

"Silence," Lucius cut off the aid who attempted to answer the question.

"Have the Praetorian Guard enter the outer chamber

after Uther enters my court. They are to enter silently. I do not want that man to know that I have risen to the occasion and wised up to his nefarious plan. He thinks he is smarter than me. Who does he think I am? I am after all the man who outsmarted him and took the throne from his hands. I am indeed smarter than him."

"Yes, sire. Your Highness is indeed the smartest monarch in all the world. Uther Pendragon has nothing to offer in comparison to you. "

"How many men does he have in the city?"

"Spies tell us that he has none."

"Your spies are either incompetent or are loyal to him."

"No, sire. These spies have a vested interest in seeing you remain as emperor."

"Yet they say that Uther has no forces in the city. Where are the bulk of his forces then?"

"They are split in two, just as it has always been. He has one legion at the garrison in Verona—just over five thousand men. It is commanded by his son, Arthur. He also has a second legion in Genua. The rumor is that he is raising a third."

"We cannot allow him to raise a third. How many men do we have?"

"We have no legions in the north aside from Uther's. The legion in Florentia now resides just outside Rome."

"How many men do we have there?"

"Less than five thousand, sire."

"In the south?"

"In the south, we have none, but we have another five thousand men in Ostia. All the other garrisons had been vacated and the men returned to Rome. Half of them have been elevated to the Praetorian Guard and the rest have been placed in Neapolis together with the naval force."

"How many men in total?"

"Including the Guard, we have no more than fifteen thousand men."

"And Uther has just over ten thousand?"

"Yes, sire. But that is not an advantage. Uther's men, the ones under his son Arthur and the ones under his best friend, Cassius, are highly trained. Five thousand men under Arthur carry the weight of ten thousand men under one of our generals."

"Rubbish. I have seen our men fight. I sit on this throne because of the way our men fought."

"No, sire. You sit on the throne, with all due respect, because Uther decided not to contest your challenge. If he had commanded his forces in Genua and Verona to descend on Rome, we would have lost."

"I do not believe that, Titus. And you would be a fool to believe it yourself. I won because I combined intelligence with strength and bravery. He lost because he was weak. Enough of this talk. If you think he is such a threat then the way to protect the throne, in addition to fortifying the city with more troops, is to cut off the head of the troops in the north."

Titus shuddered at the thought of what his emperor

was suggesting. Titus was a smart man, having once been in the employ of Uther Pendragon himself. He had learned much from his old master and learned nothing from his current employer. He was in the best place to compare the two men and found the latter wanting.

"Sire, killing him would only enrage his son who may not be as wise as his father, but makes up for it in ferocity. The legions are loyal to the son as much as they are to the father. You cannot kill Uther. Uther knows this. That is why he walks into the palace without bodyguards to protect him."

"The insolence," Lucius sneered.

"Sire, killing him will also turn the tide of loyalty in many of the men in our ranks. He holds great respect with them."

"But they're loyal to me!" Lucius shouted.

"Only because Uther yielded. They would have fought for you to the death, but over time they would not have loved you the same way Uther's men love him."

"If I can't kill him, then I will lock him up in the dungeons."

"Under what charge, sire?"

"You sound as if you are against me, Titus."

"I am not against you, sire."

"If you are not with me—not enthusiastic about every move I make—that means you are against me," the usurper snarled as he poured the wine from the goblet into his gullet, unsightly in his execution.

Titus sighed softly, knowing that his emperor's actions were about to put in motion a chain of events that he could not anticipate, and his emperor did not even consider. If only Uther were here, he would be able to see down the chain of consequences and tell the idiot on the throne what would happen next, Titus thought.

"Send him in, and once I find him guilty, have the guards take him into custody and take that wife of his into custody as well."

"No, sire. You must not do that. If you take his wife into custody, nothing would stop Arthur from raining down on Rome with fire and fury."

Lucius grew more impatient than he had already been. He just could not shake the Pendragon family no matter how hard he tried. There was always something forcing him into taking a different action.

"No. My orders stand. Send a dozen Praetorian Guards to Uther's house. Tell them to wait for the signal. Once they see a flaming arrow launched from the northern spire, they are to arrest her and take her to Ostia. Hold her there without anyone's knowledge. No one will dare attack while I have Uther and Igraine in my clutches."

"Very well, sire," Titus replied, sad on the inside at how the events of the morning had transpired. He had supported Lucius because he wanted more power and wealth, something that Uther was not interested in and didn't appreciate. That was the only reason Titus left Uther's side. His reward had been considerable. But by taking the land in the south of Italy, and the palatial home inside Rome, he had signed away his soul to the devil.

As he walked away from the emperor, each clap the sole of his sandals made on the granite floor sent a bolt of lightning through him. Each marked a moment closer to the perilous sequence of events that would soon unfold if this plan were to be executed.

C.J. BROWN

7

KRAMPUS REROUTED

JUST BEFORE THE REMAINING LIFE slipped out with the last of Adolphus' breath, Arthur realized that there were better uses for the barbarian general than his death could ever accomplish. Arthur released his pressure off of Adolphus' neck as he slipped into unconsciousness. Arthur got up and looked around to see if any Hun had noticed. None had. He looked to the leeward side as the massive horde hurtled to the village below. The expendables had already reached the city and so had the commander and the captains that had chased them from behind. The bulk of the barbarian army, led by the evil Krampus, had almost reached the foothills. There was no way they could make it back up anytime soon.

With that, Arthur gave the order to his men in the shade of the trees. At once the soldiers on foot began their charge as the Huns in the plains were taken by shock. But these were no daffodils. They were hardened men of war. Whatever shock and awe that overcame them, did so only for a fleeting moment. It didn't take long for them to collect their wits and their axes and respond to the attacking Romans.

As the Huns in the clearing turned to the Roman footsoldiers in the east, Arthur's archers and cavalry waited behind the western treeline until the full might of the Huns committed themselves to the incoming attack. Once they had, the archers hidden in the trees let loose their arrows. From a distance, Arthur could see it rain down on the rear ranks of the Huns, now focused ahead on the eastern assault.

Row by row, the Huns fell with arrows in their backs until they thinned out in number. When enough barbarians had fallen, the arrows ceased their assault. The soldiers in the east continued to slay the Huns with their swords, now with significantly lesser repercussions as the Hun ranks collapsed. With no more arrows falling from the heavens, Arthur's cavalry began its charge from the southwest treeline. Pinned in between and with no help from their comrades on the leeward side, the Huns realized they were trapped. What's worse, they had no one to lead them out of trouble.

The cavalry plowed through, thundering across the

field, coming up on the backs of the Huns confused by the sudden turn of events. Each Roman blade landed on the neck of a Hun, and then another, and then another. Each swing connected with the intended target and separated every man from his head with great prejudice. Before long, the muddy soil turned crimson and the field on the backward slope was rid of every last barbarian.

Arthur still had one more part of the plan to execute. Leaping onto his horse, he flung his hand in the direction of the catapults as his men watched him, anticipating his next command. The six archers who had expertly brought down the flagmen joined his heels and together they took flight toward the two dozen trebuchets just behind the ridge. Another two dozen horsemen ascended the backward slope to join him, and together they recalibrated the catapults.

Arthur knew the exact distances he needed the fireballs to fly and guided his men on what to do.

On the slope, almost reaching the plains, the advancing horde, a hundred paces behind the expendables, growled with glee at the prospect of sacking the city. Instead, they began to witness fireballs descend in front of them, cutting off their advance and separating them from the expendables.

Krampus growled in anger as he came to a grinding halt and turned to look at the hill. The rain had all but stopped and the sun on the eastern ridge began to illuminate the land below with greater luminosity. He looked up to find that Adolphus was not where he was supposed to be. The fireballs had stopped but the attack had dealt a severe blow. Their path to Verona had been blocked and going around it would put them face to face with the garrison. But to Krampus, it did not matter. He just wanted his blood for the day. If the fools at the catapults had made a mistake, he thought, he was not about to be the beneficiary of that error. He would still have his blood for the day. Looking to his left and to his right, he contemplated the shorter route around the blazing plains.

Determining that the eastern route was better off, he charged with his men in tow and they rounded the edge of the burning fields and straight toward the quiet fortress.

8

COWARDICE IN THE FLESH

"THE EMPEROR WILL SEE YOU now, Uther," Titus uttered with the necessary firmness in his voice.

"Greetings, Titus. How are you, old friend?" Uther responded, knowing full well, from the look in Titus' eyes, that something was afoot. Uther, a silent man, would not ordinarily have extended a greeting to a man like Titus, but he needed to hear the secrets that would be contained in the timber of his voice, to ascertain the man's true thoughts.

Silence was the only response Titus could muster.

The demeanor of the response spoke volumes, even if

the words were not enough to say anything of importance. Uther studied the man but also knew that there was nothing he could do about it. His own spies had already alerted him to the increasing disdain the emperor had—all fueled by the usurper's own fear and cowardice.

So be it, Uther thought. He was already prepared for all that could take place. The doors to the emperor's receiving court were just as Uther remembered them. He had grown up amongst these walls and arches which he now passed as a stranger.

"Hail Caesar," Uther said as he presented himself in front of Lucius. "May the gods shower their blessings over your empire."

"Welcome, Uther. How goes it?"

"All is well, sire, I am happy to report."

"And how is that pretty wife of yours?"

"You are too kind, sire. My wife is well. She sends her blessings and well-wishes."

"It is received well, Uther. You may tell her that I wish her well. And, your son, Arthur. How is that young man of yours?"

"Arthur is well. It has been an entire season since I last saw him. But I get word often that he is doing well as he serves in the garrison that protects your empire, sire."

"We are pleased, Uther. Now, to what do we owe this visit?"

"Sire, the northern garrisons need to be supplemented. My plan is to raise two more legions. One will be located with our existing forces in Verona. The other will be placed in Mediolanum."

"Four legions, Uther. That is a powerful force, and all under one man. I am sure some of the senators might be disturbed by the amount of power that they may feel you are amassing."

"Those senators are not warriors like you and me, sire. They do not understand what it takes to defend an empire."

"This is true, Uther. This is true," Lucius repeated.

"My spies tell me—"

"You have spies, Uther?"

"Indeed, sire. All in service of the empire."

"Tell me, Uther, where are your spies located?"

"Primarily in Germania, sire."

"You do not have any in Rome? Within the walls of the palace? In my court?" Lucius posed, with sarcasm thick in his voice.

Uther could see that the emperor was now looking for an excuse to execute his plan.

"No, sire. My spies, my armies, and my breath are all in service of Rome and whoever sits on the throne."

"Enough, Uther. Do you take me for a fool?"

Uther did, but this would not be the right time to reveal that truth.

"Sire, I am in your service. I implore you to put aside any hostility you think exists between us, and focus on the invading armies of the north. The tribes of Germania, especially the Huns, have a deep-seated hatred for us and our way of life. The tribes in the north, the Visigoths in the west, and the Ostrogoths in the east also harbor aspirations for that chair, sire," he said, pointing to the throne. "As of yet, they have not formed an alliance, but they will soon come to the conclusion that an alliance would be the only way to bring down the banners of Rome from our walls. When they come upon that conclusion, two garrisons in the north will not be enough to hold them back."

"Are you threatening me? Is that a veiled threat?"

Uther squinted his disapproval. Everything he had said was true. There was an alliance in the offing in the north. It was not a possibility, it was a certainty—only the timing of such an event was unclear. The emperor's games were placing Rome in jeopardy and that was something that Uther could not understand or excuse.

Outside, without Uther's knowledge, two hundred Praetorian Guards assembled. Looking over his shoulder, Lucius eyed Titus at the entrance of the chamber, thirty paces behind Uther. Titus gave the signal that the guards had assembled.

"I consider this to be a threat to the emperor. This is sedition," Lucius barked.

A calm Uther said nothing at first, then lowered his voice for effect, then spoke.

"It is typically a tyrant who uses the whip of sedition to silence his perceived enemies."

"You mock your emperor?"

"It is not mockery to speak the truth. Tyrants in history

now, and I am certain, in the future, who do not have the legitimacy to govern or the mandate to rule, will use the charge of sedition as their reason for tyrannical acts."

"I am the emperor," Lucius barked once more. "You will give me the respect that that entails."

"I do sire. I am not challenging your authority. In fact, all evidence points to the contrary. I am here to seek your permission to build the armies in the north so that the invading barbarians will have significant resistance when they mount an assault."

"Or," Lucius shouted, "you raise the army to storm Rome. And that is sedition."

"It was never my intention, and never will be in the future. Rome is more than just marble and gravel. It is more than the people and the daily routine they engage in. Rome is an idea that extends beyond the life of any one man. I have sworn an oath to protect that, whether on the throne or on horseback."

"So you do not deny you feel like that seat belongs to you?"

Uther paused. It was a trick question. He was well aware that others were within earshot of the conversation and that they would be used as evidence of his guilt. Uther had to be careful with what he said and how he said it.

"No, sire. I do not want that throne. But whoever shall sit upon it shall command my loyalty and obedience... up to a point."

"Hah! So you admit there is a limit to your loyalty to the emperor."

"No, sire. Only to those who are fools. If you are a fool, then you can rightfully claim that you do not have my loyalty. But if you are not a fool, you can be sure that my sword is yours to command and my breath, yours to take."

Uther had placed him in a vice. To arrest him now meant conceding he was a fool, and whoever was behind him, Uther thought, would be witness to that. But even Uther had misjudged the limits to the emperor's stupidity and the unbridled fear he had for the might and mind of Uther Pendragon.

"This is treason. Guards!" he called.

9

INTERROGATION

Arthur and seven men returned to the high point on the ridge. The bound and gagged Adolphus remained unconscious in the mud. Stripped of his fur, the cold had turned his pale naked body a blue tinge. He didn't know it yet, but this was the first part of his interrogation.

Arthur watched from above as Krampus led his men around the blaze and to the garrison. It would not be long before the invading barbarians would arrive at the fortress's gates. From the ridge, he gave the command to his men on horseback and on foot to begin the return to the fortress. They no longer needed to take the circuitous route back.

They could all, the cavalry and the foot soldiers, return by the eastern path.

Adolphus's horse meandered in the bush, not far from its master. Arthur pointed to it and the soldier immediately understood what needed to be done. He brought it over and Arthur commanded that the general be bent over his horse. In moments all of them were on the trail once more, in pursuit of their comrades that had gone before them.

***

At the garrison, Captain Albus, a soldier deeply loyal to Uther, held the fort. He and the one thousand men of Romulus Company hid in the underground catacombs of the fortress. Here they waited for the invading barbarians that were sure to strike. Five thousand barbarians against one thousand Romans. Any military strategist would have multiplied that number by three to account for the brutal nature of the barbarians. But Arthur was resolute. He knew that these one thousand men when hiding in the subterranean passages of the garrison would be able to vanquish the unsuspecting invaders.

Arriving at the garrison, Krampus stopped short of the twenty-foot walls. There was no activity on the battlements. No archers in the crenelations, and no soldiers on the parapets. Silence reigned over the front line of the barbarian forces. Krampus, not as smart as a Roman general nor as stupid as a barbarian soldier, figured that it was a trap. He just couldn't figure out what the trap was supposed to do or how it would play out.

Disappointed with the turn of events he commanded the soldiers to raid the garrison for whatever may have been left behind. They piled in through the main entrance and filled the main yard of the Roman outpost. Everywhere they raided, they found food, clothes, coins, and other treasures they could plunder.

A trap had been set in the time the other two companies had ridden for the passes and now they waited. The fires of the night had gradually extinguished and they smoldered in the drizzle that had reached the garrison. None of the heavy rain that had pelted the leeward and backward side of the ridge had made it to the southeast corner of Verona's countryside.

Deciding that they were not about to go empty-handed for their effort, he let his men loose to scavenge the rest of the empty garrison. Many of the dormitories were locked and bolted. A few were open, and in them, they found gold and valuables. The men centered their efforts around these buildings. All five thousand men had congregated in the center of the courtyard as the men in the catacombs waited for the opportune moment. Without the barbarians realizing it, the main gates were closed from the access in the subterranean vault. One by one the gates closed and locked much to the surprise of the Huns inside.

"Break these doors down!" Krampus shouted.

The men tried to ram the doors down but to no avail. These were heavy doors of iron and timber that mere fighting swords and axes were not able to put even a dent in. As they figured out what to do they heard the sound of galloping horses in the distance. More than two thousand horsemen at full gallop were no more than a hundred paces when the Huns first heard them. Behind them were another two thousand men in a rapid march. They would arrive later but with the manner in which the Huns were trapped, foot soldiers were not needed. Gradually, men from the catacombs began to appear on the parapets. Archers surrounded the walls of the courtyard and the walls that extended into the rest of the garrison.

The Huns had lost all advantage as the Romans had used the secret passages to get from the catacombs to the top of the walls. Krampus could see men filling the drains with oil and archers now stood in their place. Within minutes, fire reigned down on the helpless soldiers, as they were commanded to let loose all the arrows on every single Hun.

***

"You have no army left, Adolphus. All you have now is your life. Is your silence worth your life?" Arthur asked the bound man.

In an attempt to free himself, he jerked at his binds only to find that they had not been tied by an amateur.

"Let me go, Roman."

"I think not. I think I will ransom you to your king. How much would I be able to fetch for you?"

The thought of being the bargaining chip for a ransom

trade did not appeal to a man who had been driven by pride all his life.

"My king will pay nothing for me."

"I think you are lying. He is not a stupid man. He knows loyalty when he sees it. He must surely see it in you. For that loyalty, I am certain he will pay."

Adolphus could not explain to him that Attila never paid for hostages. And if he ever got them back, he always killed them as an example to the other men to not get captured. Adolphus was now stuck between being traded or being killed. In front of him were two giant Romans, eager to tear him from limb to limb.

"That is enough talk," Arthur suddenly boomed. "I no longer have any patience for this." His voiced bounced off the stone walls of the torture room. The room was built especially to extract information from enemy combatants. In it, there were all manner of tools that were used to torture the prisoner.

Turning to the giants at the end of the room, he nodded his head backward to signal his approval for the next action they were to take.

Without hesitation, the two men unbound Adolphus and secured his hands to ropes that came from holes in the wall on either side. Adolphus had no idea where those ropes led or what they were attached to beyond the wall. Once both the ropes were tied, the men tapped the wall until the ropes pulled his arms snug.

"What will you do? Crucify me?"

Arthur didn't say a word. Crucifixion was a common Roman punishment, but this was not a punishment. However, Arthur did not feel like he needed to explain the intricacies of Roman crucifixion. He stood in front of Adolphus and stared him in the eye.

"I only have one question for you. If you answer that, I will set you free."

Adolphus was starting to see that Arthur was not a man to be trifled with.

"What is your question, Roman?"

"That I cannot tell you."

"If you don't tell me how do I answer?"

"You have to guess. If you don't guess the right question and proceed to answer it, then I am afraid this conversation will end."

Arthur tapped the wall and Adolphus could feel the ropes pull from both sides and his arms stretched.

"When Alexander the Great was betrayed, or when he was lied to, he would strap a man to a pair of bent trees, tied his limbs to them and released the trees. Do you know what happened to the man?"

Adolphus could imagine. He too had studied the history of Alexander the Great. He knew what the Roman was talking about and he now guessed what his hands were tied to."

"Tell me what you want to know. I will tell you."

"Like I said. I only need one question answered. If you tell me that, I will let you go. You can run back to your kin or disappear into the forests, I don't care. But if you don't tell me, then you shall feel what traitors to Alexander felt."

"King Attila will be here in three days. That's what you want to know, yes?"

"I already know that," Arthur said, lying to his prisoner's face.

"He is at the head of ten thousand men."

"I already know that too," Arthur replied, feigning impatience.

This went on all night until everything Arthur needed to know had been answered by the Hun General.

"You have still not answered the one question I need and I am tired of this game. He looked one last time at the bewildered Hun and tapped the wall. This time the tap was four consecutive taps, and the rope eased back until Adolphus's arms were able to fall to his sides. The rope loosened until he heard galloping horses. Two galloping horses. The rope remained on the ground but two horses had been dispatched, now riding at top speed. All of a sudden, the ropes snapped his arms off the sides and ripped it off his shoulders, much to the excruciating pain of the general who fell to the ground, free from his binds, dying soon after.

C.J. BROWN

10

NEWS FROM ROME

"**M**Y LORD, A RIDER FROM Rome. He requests a moment of your time." Arthur raised his eyes to look at his valet announce the visitor. The fire in the hearth raged, in the room as Arthur sat planning his next steps.

"From my father?"

"Doesn't seem to be."

"Fine. Send him in."

A man exhausted from swift passage appeared before the general. "My lord, I bring news."

"How is the moon over Rome?"

The rider paused for a minute, remembering that all messages between Rome and Arthur carried a coded phrase. In the rush of the moment, he had forgotten. Recomposing himself, he took a deep breath and searched his memory.

"There's no moon tonight, my lord, only stars and three clouds."

"Proceed with the message, rider."

"My lord," the man said, straightening his composure to match the seriousness of the message he was about to deliver, "your father has been arrested by the emperor."

"What news of my mother?" Arthur immediately questioned.

"Your mother is on her way north, but via a circuitous route that I am not privy to. She moved early yesterday morning before Lord Uther went to see the emperor."

"What charges were brought against my father?"

"Sedition, my lord."

"The coward is charging my father with sedition?" Arthur yelled. He crossed his arms over his chest and narrowed his eyes. "What else?"

"When they couldn't find your mother at home, they burnt it down and a legion of five thousand men were dispatched to take you into custody. If you do not come, they have orders to kill you."

"When did they leave Rome?"

"They are not coming from Rome. They were dispatched from Ostia."

Arthur pondered the developments.

Why now? he wondered. He had no way of answering that question with the accuracy it deserved.

"Where are they holding my father?"

"He is in Carcer Tullanium."

"Are you certain?"

"Yes, my lord. Why?"

"If they have put him there, it means they do not plan to keep him alive for long. Is there any other news?"

"Not news, but a rumor."

Arthur looked on with suspicion. The facts were already weighing heavily against him. Did he want to hear a rumor that might be a distraction?

"What is it?" he asked, the tone of his question giving the flavor of suspicion to his rider.

"My lord, forgive me. This is a rumor but I would not bring it up if it did not rise to the occasion of being important. A rider is also being dispatched to Genua."

"To what end?"

"They plan to tell them that you and your father are traitors and they will be given the choice to pledge their allegiance to the emperor. Those who decline will be killed."

That news complicated matters even more.

Arthur raised his eyes, looked at the rider, then reached into his side pocket and retrieved two gold coins. "For your trouble, rider. Spend the night, then ride to Ravenna. That will keep you out of the path of the legion that is on its way here. Avoid them at all costs, and stay out of Rome."

"My lord, if I may."

"Speak your mind, rider."

"Let me come with you, my lord. I have nothing in Rome. I beg you, please let me come with you."

"Get some rest. I will leave word with the commander what I decide. My answer will be with him by the time you wake up."

"Thank you, my lord."

Arthur returned to studying the maps. Everything he had planned now needed to be changed. Attila, the King of the Huns, was barreling across from the east at the head of ten thousand men, according to Adolphus. He would arrive in less than two days. But that was no longer the most important issue. Neither was the fact that five thousand Romans were ascending the peninsula en route to Verona.

The biggest issue now was Uther. If he didn't get to his father in time, it would get harder to rescue him. Lucius's plan was no big secret. He would have to kill Arthur first and disband the legion before he could kill Uther. If he missed that step and rushed to stick a dagger in the old general's back, all hell would break loose and a civil war would ensue. Even Lucius was not that stupid to overlook that, Arthur thought.

"Vipsanius," Arthur called out to his trusted captain and friend who was standing just beyond the walls of Arthur's quarters.

"Yes, my lord."

"Send twelve men to intercept the messenger that is headed to Genua. Then proceed to Genua and have the men take the coastal route down to Ostia. They should be there in a week. Have them wait there."

"Yes, my lord. What about the rest of us?"

"We will move Germina Maxima by nightfall to Ravenna. The praetor is an ally of my father's. He will join our fight. His triremes will be enough to move all our men to Ostia. With the tides the way they are now, it will take us seven days to get to Ostia, undetected."

Vipsanius nodded. Arthur had thought the plan through. Lucius would never consider that both Uther's armies would attack from Ostia. It would be the side of Rome—the one that faced the port city of Ostia—that he would leave unprotected.

By daybreak of the following morning, with a legion loyal to Lucius still at least five days away, Arthur began the arduous task of repositioning his men. He had stopped thinking of his father and what may have become of him. It was a distraction he could not afford. There was no room for error now. If he did not succeed, Uther would die. If he overplayed his hand, Uther would die. If he was too late, all his men would die. The peril was high, and Arthur was alone in making the decisions.

C.J. BROWN

11

ATTILA THE HUN

AS THE FIRST SNOW OF winter fell, the barbarian horde began the final leg of their journey. Ten thousand men and two thousand expendables marched east toward Verona on a journey that would take three days. There were small hamlets along the way, none, however, worth sacking.

At the head of twelve thousand souls, the king of the Hun tribe, Attila, sat perched on his draft horse. Trained to transport the king, the breed of horse that was normally used to drag and plow the fields had a strong back and thick legs. Attila's stables were filled with draft horses bred expressly for one of the heaviest men in all of Germania.

Attila was impatient. A fowl mood hung around him

as the soldiers got underway. Sitting bare-chested, high on his beast, he didn't care that he presented himself as the obvious target of any archer hiding behind the tree lines. His dreadlocks, thick and long, fell past his shoulders and covered some of the ink and scars that decorated his sunburnt skin. Each drawing and every scar told a story about his life and the history of his tribe.

Before Attila, the Huns were nomadic, roaming from one land to another, picking up different groups as they moved. Mostly rejects of communities, people who could not belong in more established towns, joined these nomadic travelers. Over time, the population of the migratory culture grew and resources to provide for their lifestyle dried up rapidly wherever they went.

To the farmers and merchants along the way, the Huns were like locusts, damaging the crops everywhere they went. Gradually, the Huns were detested and fought off everywhere they went. Organically, they grew from roamers to marauders. As marauders, they organized under a King and became soldiers. The increased ability brought with it a heightened sense of greed. The greediest of all tribal leaders, Attila pointed to the lands south of the Alps and questioned why the Romans had more wealth than his people. And he told them that the gods did not approve.

"I am the chosen one," he had claimed to his people. "The gods have chosen me to lead our people south and harvest their crops, eat their food, wear their clothes, and

MERLIN'S TOMB

live like them. Follow me. Fight with me. And we will fulfill the command of the gods."

Every address he gave his people, the message was the same until men, women, and children, motivated by greed, saw Attila as the only one who could satisfy their longing while fulfilling the command of the gods.

Now, at the height of his rule and at the cusp of victory, this was to be the journey that finally led to the success that he desired. Twenty thousand men waited for him and his ten thousand. It was a sizable army that had taken a lifetime to build, and would now be able to vanquish the northern legion in the east. From there, marching down to Rome would be child's play, Attila believed.

As he inched closer to Verona, his army, five men wide and two thousand ranks long, stretched a league behind him. Catapults and weapons, pulled by thousands of men, moved slowly, making the short distance between the two towns a three-day affair.

They ate while they marched, and stopped only to sleep between the hours of midnight and dawn. No camps were erected for rest. They slept on the road where they stopped, then arose and continued marching. Not a second was wasted. The gods' will was at hand.

As they marched, Attila prepared his mind for battle. He envisioned one face—the man he would battle to the death. It was a face he had dreamt about for a decade. It was the face of the man who had slain his wife and children and made Attila a king without a bloodline. It was the face of Rome's greatest general and the man who should have been the emperor—Uther Pendragon.

Revenge had fueled Attila's plans. When he first developed the idea of sacking Rome, it was purely because he assumed that it would be Uther on the throne by the time he got there. But since then, Uther had been cheated out of the throne. He couldn't change his objective, and in fact, vanquishing the vain and foolish Lucius would be easier, he thought.

"Riders approaching, my lord," Bishkar shouted, breaking his train of thought.

Attila exited his dream and focused on the road ahead. Dawn had shed enough light to be able to see a full league down the straight path.

"Continue moving," Attila replied. Inside, he wondered what news the riders brought. They were one of theirs. The colors waving above them promised that much. Attila believed that it was news from Adolphus. A pragmatic man when he needed to be, he determined that this would not be good news as Adolphus would have waited to share good tidings. This was a warning of some sort.

"My lord—"

"Sire!" Attila shouted. "I am not your lord. I am your king."

The man on the horse shook himself out of the sudden daze the loud and booming voice had placed him.

"A thousand apologies, sire. The road is long and I had to move swiftly to reach. I am not from your tribe."

MERLIN'S TOMB

"In time for what?"

"General Arthur asked me to deliver a message."

"Who is General Arthur and why do I care about his message?"

"Arthur, son of Uther, general of Germina Maxima, protector of the Limes Germanicus, servant of the emperor Lucius is the sender of the message and you should care about the message because, in his kindness, he wishes to spare the life of the army behind you. Twelve thousand men, is it not?"

Attila was not liking this messenger who had a strange arrogance that permeated his pale skin and slapped Attila in the face. Before Attila could respond, another of the riders behind the lead, led a horse toward the front and handed it to one of the Huns. It carried two bloody sacks on both sides of the saddle.

Attila looked at it, his nose pointed a shade above the horizon, his jaws clenched in anger. For as greedy and vindictive as he was, Attila was not a foolish man. He was a brilliant tactician, second only to Uther in his prime. By the shape of the carpetbags, he could tell what it was.

A nod to Bishkar told the apprentice what he needed to do. Bishkar had been by Attila's side ever since they had started on the quest to quash Rome. He bided his time with respect to Adolphus' esteemed position in the tribe but knew that one day it would be his turn to lead the armies of Attila and perhaps take over from the man who had no heir.

Bishkar dismounted from his steed and took possession of the horse he recognized to be Adolphus'. The bags, seeped in crimson emanated a stench that only attracted vultures and maggots. It was putrid, and now clear what was inside would be disturbing. Bishkar hoisted the bag off the horse's left and threw it on the ground, then untied the rope that secured it. An arm and a torso fell out. Maggots populated most of the contents of the package, still too young to fly.

The second package on the other side of the saddle contained the rest of the person including the head. What was still recognizable, identified the body to the king— General Adolphus. Anger erupted within his chest as he considered revenge upon the riders who had delivered the message.

Bishkar could see the thoughts that swirled in his king's head and knew that that would not be the best way to go. Before Attila could say anything, Bishkar rose to the occasion and dispatched the riders from the king's sight.

"You have delivered your message. Leave now. We have no response to your master."

The riders understood that even a moment's hesitation would determine the fate of their lives and turned their horses and took to the wind.

"Bishkar!" Attila boomed. "Dispatch a dozen riders to follow those men and see where they go. The rest of you, resume the march!" he shouted.

"Yes, sire."

"And when you are done, bury the remains of our friend. I shall continue marching forward. Join me when he is in the ground."

It wasn't until the winter sun was at its zenith when Bishkar returned to his king's side and reported that Adolphus had been buried and a stone placed as a marker for the location. Many of the Huns had been buried in the same way, as it was the nomadic way. Dying en route was not a rare event.

C.J. BROWN

12

INTO THE CITY

THE LEGION LOYAL TO LUCIUS arrived in Verona to find the city burned to the ground and the forest beyond scorched. The townsfolk told of invading hordes and no Romans to protect them. Arriving at the garrison, the men found thousands of decaying and burnt corpses stripped of their clothes.

It was easy to deduce that the legion had been decimated by the invading horde who had then stolen all the valuables. Fresh snow the night before made it difficult to track which direction the horde proceeded to. Riders were sent to villages and hamlets just south of Verona only to be told that no horde was seen. But a horde of ten thousand men, it seems, were encamped in the seaside town of Patavium, in the southeast.

"That must be the horde that did our work for us," the commander chided to his lieutenant.

"Should we go and thank them?" the lieutenant replied, jokingly.

"The two men looked at each other, realizing that they would return to Rome as heroes of the empire and be rewarded for vanquishing the emperor's enemies. They just had to word their report correctly. By neglecting to tell the emperor of the horde, they would be the heroes.

***

Within eight days, the men of Felix Fortis, on foot, and the men of Gemina Maxima, by sea, assembled in unprecedented numbers just twenty leagues from the imperial city of Rome. Uther Pendragon was now on his tenth day of capture. Not a morsel of food had passed his lips. He feared an attempt to poison him. On the third day of his capture, he had grown accustomed to the fast. After the eighth, he had lost his vigor and energy. But he knew that his fate would not be relegated to the men who served obsequiously to the usurper.

Lucius only had one full legion at his disposal and he had sent that one to deal with Arthur. In the city, he had five thousand Praetorian Guards to protect him—all had sworn allegiance to him, and him alone—not the throne. In the days after arresting Uther and finding out that an essential cog to his plan could not be found, he realized that the army was at a disadvantage. Only the news of the legion in Verona alleviated his concerns. But still, he thought, the time to kill Uther was not yet at hand.

Lucius praised himself when holding court, telling whoever would listen that he had gotten the best of Uther and his men. His rule over Rome was now certain and secured. All the while, Titus looked upon him, knowing deep in his heart that all was not well.

Until he could see Uther's body laying on the granite of the palace alongside his wife and his son, nothing was certain. Titus knew that Igraine had allies in the provinces and Arthur was not as easily killed as Lucius thought he would be. He tried to relay that concern to the emperor, but Lucius was too buried within his own fantasy to see that all was not yet in the clear.

***

On the night of the black moon, precisely a fortnight after they had vanquished the invading barbarians, Arthur stood at the head of ten thousand men.

"We are about to commit the gravest of crimes. A legion of Rome has never entered the city in three hundred years. If we are caught, every last one of us will be killed. Our families will be sold into slavery, and all the wealth we have acquired will be forfeited by the emperor," Arthur began.

On this dark night, the heir to the Pendragon legacy was dressed in black. No armor and no greaves. Just a black tunic and a black cape to shield him from the cold.

"We are a hundred paces from the palace. But that is not our objective. Our only objective is the rescue of my father—your general. Remember, he was the man who brought you into this legion. He was the man that held his tongue when the throne was usurped from him. He was the man who pledged allegiance to the city and the Empire and not to the man who pretends to be the emperor. Lucius is nobody. He is not our target. You all know what you have to do. Let us begin."

With that, Arthur and a dozen archers began their excursion into the city. Hiding in the shadows, they made their way to the Colosseum. The smell of blood hung in the air. Men fought and died on the mighty stages of the largest edifice known to man. It was also the best way to enter the subterranean system of tunnels and catacombs that led to the prison in the north.

The tunnels ran alongside dungeons that smelled of death and pain. Many men groaned while others whimpered. Still, others yelled and screamed. It was the worst deprivation of the human condition Arthur had ever seen. It was the thing that made him ashamed of being Roman. If he one day ascended to the throne that was rightfully his father's, and then his, he would knock down the dungeons and fill the edifice with a foundation to build a large library atop of it as Alexander had done in Egypt.

Arthur moved quickly, not thinking of the distance and the peril that lay before him. His men, two legions of highly trained warriors, sworn to protect Rome, stood behind him in the shadows, waiting for a signal. All he had to do was send a red flare into the night sky and they would descend upon Rome with the fury of a wounded beast. But he knew better than to unleash that power. There was a reason no commander had ever entertained the possibility of bringing troops into the city.

If he did so now and overthrew the emperor, someone would be able to do it again. But it wasn't his own seat on the throne he was worried about. A throne that was up for grabs just by the might of a larger army meant that no ruler would be able to focus on the welfare of the people. That was the reason for peace and the reason for strong legions on the border.

Arthur believed peace to be the ultimate reason for a strong army. It was also the reason that he brought the men to the gates of the city but didn't want to use them unless he absolutely had to. For now, rescuing his father was the only goal on his mind. He would then think about reuniting with his mother, and then the three of them would plan the next steps together.

An hour later, he found himself exactly where he had entered the underground passages. The darkness and the maze-like structure had turned him around and wasted valuable time. Arthur realized that this would not be the best path to bring his father through. He stopped to think, while one of the soldiers behind him could no longer hold his gut, and vomited in torrents.

Thinking back, he realized where he had made the

mistake and how they had circled back to the start. Now they had to increase the pace and push forward toward the prison complex. As a failsafe measure, there was a cut-off time that the men were given. In the event they did not see the flare or Arthur had not yet returned, they were to descend on the city at dawn—four hours from the time they had left—and foment an uprising. This was different from the red flare that would signal an attack on the city. Now there were only three hours left. Having the army attack while he was still in the tunnels would unleash a series of consequences that were catastrophic.

Disregarding the discomfort of the environment, Arthur pushed forward, going through the same passages he had an hour earlier. This time he moved faster, less distracted by the sights, sounds, and smell. The men arrived at the junction where they had made the wrong turn and stopped. Looking at each other, everyone's eyes were in agreement. They were to take the passage that led to the left. No one spoke even though they had all wrapped their faces with the cape they had brought along. It was more to shield their noses than to hide their faces.

With the passage of the next hour, they arrived at the edge of the Colosseum complex and circumvented the junction they knew there would be guards. The Carcer Tullanium was one league from their original starting point at the south side of the Colosseum.

"We are running out of time, my lord," one of the

archers said, grabbing Arthur's hand and bringing the problem to his attention.

"I know. There is nothing we can do but pick up the pace. We have to hurry," Arthur suggested.

By the time they reached the outer wall of the Carcer Tullanium, it was almost dawn.

***

"Commander," the archer called out.

"What is it, soldier?"

"It is dawn. There is light over the horizon."

Vipsanius grew concerned. He was afraid of this moment. Unlike the men under his command, he understood the ramifications of the action he was about to order.

"We are supposed to begin the attack if the general is not back with his father. Should we begin, sir?"

Even though the plan had already been laid out, the decision to go was now on his shoulders and he was not intent on going down in history as the man who called the attack on Rome.

"We will begin as soon as I give the order, soldier. Not a minute sooner. Now step back and prepare to move when I give the order."

"Yes, Commander," the soldier, following orders, responded. The men in the army had somehow been motivated to foment rebellion in the city they had sworn to protect.

In the distance, Vipsanius could hear the murmur of

men impatient to attack. But it no longer sounded like Roman legionnaires, but more like barbarian mercenaries with loot to pillage and citizens to capture.

Each second that passed, the sky above began to turn a lighter shade of blue and the men grew a darker shade of red, holding their anticipation within.

***

Reaching the outer wall of the underground vault, three stories below the streets of Rome, Arthur and his men came upon a company of guards. They had just reported for duty and were fresh and alert. Nothing short of a fight would have to be undertaken to be able to get past them. Being so far below the ground and having been lost twice since they began their trek, they had effectively lost all track of time but knew it was getting late. With the disorientation of fatigue and impatience with the foul conditions of the tunnels, they were distracted.

With time already short, Arthur had no time to ponder the consequences or the possibilities of the current challenge. They were paces away from gaining entry into the complex that held Uther. It suddenly occurred to him that the three dozen men were part of an opportunity. It was certainly an issue, but they could harvest some food from it. His decision to fight was spontaneous and the men, all thirteen of them, charged a company of the thirty-six Roman prison guards. He only had one order: "Keep one man alive. Kill the rest."

By the time they were done, it was exactly what the

men had accomplished. A fight that had lasted a good part of an hour, now way past daybreak, had yielded the only break of the mission. They now had one guard in custody.

"Where is Uther Pendragon?" Arthur insisted.

With a blade at his throat, his feigned loyalty to the emperor seemed to vanish, but not quick enough for the men who were worried about what would happen in the event the signal to cease the attack was not given in time.

As the guard hesitated, Arthur swung his blade and cut off the prisoner's right wrist, throwing the man into severe pain and shock. It was, however, enough to elevate his sense of urgency and make him point them in the direction of the cell that contained Uther Pendragon.

"Carry him. If he lies, sever his other hand," Arthur commanded in a sudden display of brutality that his men had seen only under rare conditions.

As they made their way toward the cell which was located at a higher location, their fears began to materialize. Light began to pierce the gaps in the stone walls. A cold shudder ran through Arthur. He turned to look at his men who could see the light beyond the walls of the prison.

"Where is he?" Arthur asked once more.

"Continue up the tower. Uther Pendragon is in the highest cell."

"You six, stay with him. You six, come with me," Arthur commanded and began racing up the stone steps that circled up the tower, passing cells that lined the passage. Within moments, they found Uther and liberated him from the prison that held him. He was in no condition to travel, requiring the men to carry him.

But from the tower, they could see the edges of the city that had already begun rioting. Fires burned in the French Quarter, at the southernmost extent of the city, and the melee was spreading.

"We have to leave. Now!" Arthur shouted as they began down the steps to meet the rest of the men.

***

Meanwhile back at the Imperial Palace, Titus had received word of the chaos that was unfolding across the southern part of the city and moving north.

"Sire, there is a problem outside the Circus Maximus that demands your attention," Titus said, his voice shaky and his words in a jumble.

"Leave me alone, Titus. What do I care about the street disturbances? An emperor has bigger things to think about," Lucius replied, busy attending to his figurine soldiers.

"Yes, sire. But the problem is not limited to the streets surrounding the area. It is popping up in various areas south of Capitoline."

"What do you mean?"

The southeast quarter seems to be having street demonstrations and numerous houses and government offices have been burnt. The same in the southwest. Outside Circus Maximus, the tax collector's office has been burnt, and many of the dungeon cells under the

Colosseum have been unlocked and the prisoners have been freed."

"Prisoners? What about Uther Pendragon?"

Titus fell silent.

"Well, what about that vile man?"

"He is no longer in his cell, sire."

"You didn't tell me this? This is the one news that would have made a difference and you did not tell me this?"

"I didn't want to anger you, sire."

By the time Lucius had come to know about the rescue, Arthur, Uther and the twelve men that accompanied him had raced to the coast. They were to rendezvous with their men, almost ten thousand of them, who had instigated riots, started fires, disrupted commerce, and damaged roads. But, not a single Roman was killed by the hand of Arthur's men.

C.J. BROWN

13

BISHKAR'S RISE

"**B**ISHKAR," KING ATTILA BECKONED.
"I am here, sire."
"We will camp outside the next hamlet and pause our journey."

"Yes, sire. I will make it happen."

"I have a task for you, my young apprentice."

"Anything, my lord. My will is yours to command."

"I want you to go to Verona disguised as a trader. Find out who planned the attack on my troops. Find out who killed my general. I want names."

"Yes, sire. And, where will you be?"

"Waiting for you in Patavium."

Patavium stood at the crossroads. Attila knew that if

he waited there he could do one of two things when the right moment presented itself. He could proceed to Verona where his troops had fallen or he could head directly for Rome, although the latter was less plausible with the culling of his army. The sudden blow to his numbers had set Attila back by months. Raising an army of equal strength would take at least two years—sooner if he had an able general, and with Adolphus gone, raising an army would be difficult at best. But Attila wanted to attack now. He could not wait any longer to avenge his family and now, Adolphus.

"Yes, sire. I shall leave at once."

"One more thing, Bishkar."

"Yes, sire?"

"If you are successful in this mission, I will announce you as the replacement to General Adolphus."

It was the opportunity Bishkar had been waiting for all his life. A new bounce in his step characterized his departure from Attila's side.

It would take an army two days to reach Verona but a single rider could make it in less than one. With enthusiasm fueling his stride, the sharp-witted apprentice set off. Dressed in traveling clothes, trading in his armor for fur, he departed west.

***

"I know of Arthur," Attila murmured, as Bishkar stood before him reporting the details of his mission. He had succeeded in finding out all that had happened in Verona.

It only took three days for him to ingratiate himself with the town's fold, lavishing them with money and tales of trade in the exotic east. Within a short period, he had gained all that he needed to know and a good idea of where the legion had gone.

Bishkar listened.

"He is Uther's oldest son, and heir," Attila continued, suddenly seeing opportunity inside the chaos. After a moment's consideration, he looked up and chose silence as his initial response. "You have done well. Beyond expectation, in fact. As promised, you will now lead my forces, General Bishkar."

"Thank you, sire. I shall work tirelessly to see the aspirations of my king come to fruition."

Attila nodded.

"What would you do now? Should we proceed to Rome and lay waste to it, or should we proceed to Verona?" Attila asked.

"There is nothing for us in Verona. It would be a waste of time to go there. We now hold a strategic advantage here. We should keep it. The fact that the emperor sent the legion from Ostia to attack Uther's men, means that there is an opportunity we can exploit," the new general replied.

"What if we captured Uther from prison?" Attila inquired, seeing opportunity in the situation.

"No, sire. We will not be able to succeed there and we will not be able to win a battle with our diminished forces. I suggest instead a temporary alliance," Bishkar advised.

"Never. Bishkar, you have spent a long time by my side. Do you not see that I would never forge an alliance with the Romans?" Attila was furious at the prospect.

"Yes, sire. I know you very well. But your hatred should be directed at the man who wronged you—Uther. He is now vulnerable."

"He is, and he is most vulnerable while he sits in that Roman prison."

"You can be certain that Arthur is on his way to rescue him. We should wait. Arthur has fallen so far outside the emperor's favor that he had sent an entire legion to kill him and wipe out his men. Lucius sees Arthur as a bigger threat than he sees you, sire."

"So your idea is to make use of this momentary opportunity."

Bishkar went on to outline a plan that would exact the revenge Attila wanted on Uther. The plan was more vicious and vindictive than Attila's own.

14

BLACK MOON RISING

RIDING HARD, WITH HIS FATHER in his saddle, Arthur moved swiftly to the coast. Ostia would no longer be a safe haven, Arthur knew. Heading south of Rome would be a poor tactical decision as the emperor's armies could push them south until there was nowhere to run, but into the Adriatic Sea.

North was the only way out, Arthur calculated. With this plan, the men pushed their horses to the brink of exhaustion. Knowing that Uther was in grave condition, they had to reach a safe haven and tend to him. A fortnight without food and water left him barely clinging to life and the repeated jolts of a galloping horse was not the best way to aid his recovery.

With enough distance between them, Arthur made the decision to stop at the farm of an old ally. It was run by a loyalist to the true emperor's line from Constantine. The inn had not been in the plan but would have to do for now.

They had ridden for a day and Uther, the general of the two most powerful legions in the Roman military was frail and becoming more fragile with each gallop. The innkeeper arranged for the horses to be tended to, then hidden, and the guests were shown to the basement in the barn.

"Where did you begin dragging the horse blankets?" the old man of the inn inquired. Having been a master tracker for Uther's father when he was emperor, the innkeeper knew the tricks of the trade.

"Ever since we crossed the stream," Arthur replied.

Arthur and his men had trailed the rear of their horses with horse blankets so as to drag the dust and obscure the tracks the horses made when they made their way. It was an old trick to throw off those in pursuit. But a master tracker could still read the gravel if he was even worth half his salt.

"Good, but that would not be enough. I will take care of the rest. Go and tend to your father. I will have food and water sent. Under no circumstances must you come out. Even if they burn the house down, you stay inside. They will not be able to find you in here."

"I owe you a great deal, Cassius. You have been loyal to my family for many years."

"I am loyal to the true heir of the throne, Your Highness," he said, referring to Arthur as the rightful heir to his father's throne.

"No. Please. Do not call me that. I am but my father's son, and the farther I can run from the sin of Rome, the better of a man I will be."

"And that is why, young Arthur. It is your family that needs to take back the throne and raise it up to the height it once occupied."

"I can't think of that right now, old friend. For now, I have to nurse my father to good health before leaving this place."

"So be it. We will have the opportunity to talk again. Where will you go once he is well?"

"We have allies in the north. For now, we will have to ride deep into Visigoth territory."

"We fought the Visigoths under your grandfather. They will remember your father well. I do not think they will take kindly to his presence."

"I know, but I am hoping that old wounds would have healed with time. The wound with the throne in Rome is still fresh and therefore we are better off there than we are here."

"Listen to an old man, Arthur. The Visigoths are not your friend. The Ostrogoths are allied with the Huns, which also makes them your enemy. That leaves you only hostile country between here and Paris."

Arthur looked at the old man silently. It was clear that

Arthur knew what he was doing but had not seen it fit to burden the old man with the information.

"I think I have said enough, my lord. Allow an old man to go about his business now. If you need anything, just make it known. Everything here is yours. If it was not for your grandfather, I would not have any of this. Now take this," he said, passing him two bottles. "It contains the tonic that you will need to allow your father to regain his appetite and absorb his food. The blue tonic before meals and the yellow, after."

And with that, the old man left, leaving Arthur at the entrance to the farmhouse. From the top of the mound where the barn stood, Arthur could see the expanse of the field that sloped its way gradually, then fell off the cliff into the Tyrrhenian Sea. Memories flooded his vexed mind with images of him playing in the pasture overlooking the bluest sea he could remember. It had been a time of peace that his grandfather had orchestrated.

Snapping himself out of the daze, the realization fell upon him that all that was now in the past. The feeling of clarity awoke his tired spirit and shook him out of the assumption that there was a place for him and his family on the Italian peninsula.

"No," he whispered. "No. There is no place for us among the corrupt. We have to leave this place." With a new resolve, he pulled the panel below the stall and descended the ladder beneath it. Closing the trap door behind him he proceeded down the well until reaching the bottom of the ladder where it opened out into a large cellar. The north wall of the second chamber in the cellar supported a rack that opened. It was not obvious to whoever stood in front of it. Arthur pulled on it and walked behind to a well-lit passageway, closing the panel shut behind him. Navigating the tunnels with ease, Arthur arrived at the location where his father and the twelve riders had taken refuge.

Seven days and eight nights passed and with the two tonics and a combination of nuts and cheese, Uther regained his strength—enough to get on a horse and ride north. The old man continued his visit twice a day, with fresh supplies and warm words. He would sit by Uther's side and relate old stories of Constantine III, Uther's father, and Rome's most powerful general before he became emperor.

Between the tonics, fresh cheese, and the old man's conversation, Uther raced back to the vigor Arthur was familiar with.

"Where will the men meet us?" Uther began, the morning of the eighth day.

"They will meet us on the road to Genua, a day's ride from here."

"When?"

"On the first black moon. Three days from now."

"How many men?"

"All of them. From both garrisons."

"You have done well, my son."

"Where is Mother, Father?" It was a question he had

been dying to ask his father but waited until the man was in better health.

"I have dispatched her under disguise to the north of Gaul."

"Disguise?"

"She travels with Alera."

"Just him?"

"Yes. Your mother speaks fluent Gaulish, as does Alera, which is why I chose him. They will blend in as they travel slowly. They will meet us at the edge of the Forest of Broceliande."

"When?"

"The sooner the better. But they will find a home and wait there until we arrive. Lucius has no way of knowing that is where she is headed and so she will not be in danger. But the same cannot be said for you and me."

Arthur nodded. His father's point was well taken.

"How long have we been here?" Uther asked

"Seven days, Father."

"And it has been peaceful? No attempts to find us?"

"None."

"Then we need to leave quickly, my son. If they haven't come yet, they will come soon enough. We have to ride by night and camp in the forest."

Arthur turned to the riders. "Prepare to leave tonight."

15

PEELING

IT WAS THE FIRST BLACK moon since the Riots of Rome had given cover to the escape of Uther Pendragon. The emperor's Praetorian Guards had begun to knock on every door and search every farmhouse north and west of the city. The more they searched for Uther, the more the emperor's fury grew, swearing to have all the men in Uther's legions crucified for sedition.

In the northeast, General Bishkar had already put his plan in motion. Being only a young general with little command experience did not seem to be a factor that inhibited his success. Instead, he made up for it with strategic prowess. Using spies that he developed during his trip to Verona he expanded the network and fed off the intelligence. Knowing that the emperor had spread himself thin, he convinced Attila to ride at the head of five thousand of the harshest and most vile of the warriors without the expendables in front.

Unlike Adolphus who believed in the spirit world of omens and rituals, Bishkar was a more pragmatic man—and significantly more ruthless.

"Take five thousand men with you and march into Rome from the west. It is the least protected side," Bishkar began. A plan had formed in his mind and he knew it had to be worded well if his king was to move on it.

"What will the other five thousand men do?" Attila asked.

"Send the other five thousand men with me," the general requested.

"Where will you go?" Attila had acquiesced to the plan even before it was fully described. Bishkar had put it as delicately as he needed to in a way that didn't rub the king the wrong way.

"Some of the men who were in the garrison at Verona have packed their supplies for a long journey. It looks like they are headed to Pisae or Genua. It is unlikely they will return to Genua since there is a small company of soldiers loyal to the emperor waiting to blockade them. If we find them in Pisae, we can halt their movement."

"What would be my goal with Lucius?"

"You will form an alliance—"

"What?" Attila shouted. The young man's unorthodox

ways had gone too far. Attila was not about to enter the palace of his enemy and ask for an alliance. That would be tantamount to a defeat. "I do not want to ally with that coward. I want to take the throne from under him."

"You will, sire. You will. The alliance is temporary. We have to leverage the men he has and continue to chase Arthur up the coast so that they come straight into our line.

"Once we have Arthur and his father, you can kill Lucius with your bare hands and take the throne. Arthur's legions will scatter, leaving only the three legions Lucius has, spread across all of Italy. Our ten thousand men will seem like a hundred thousand."

Attila had to agree. It was a good plan. "Proceed," he thundered. "We will do as you suggest."

***

Bishkar arrived at the hamlet where a small company of Roman soldiers had just left. Commanding his men to don the uniforms of dead legionnaires, they pretended to be Roman, although none of them, except Bishkar, spoke a word of Latin. He entered the inn and struck a conversation about the hassle the whole affair had brought about on the country. It didn't take long, with Bishkar's social skill-set, to take the innkeeper into his confidence. It wasn't long till he found out that the old man on the bluff was once under Constantine III's command.

It was all the information he needed.

Without delay, Bishkar galloped to the farm and had

his men circle the property while he strode up to the front door. In fluent Latin, he presented the master of the property with a proposition as an agent of the emperor. The old man listened, at first incredulous, then in fear of losing the comforts he had become accustomed to.

Then he listened some more. He could tell right away that the man in the uniform was not Roman. He couldn't tell if he was Visigoth or Ostrogoth, but it had to be one of the two. There was a northern look about the man. From the pallor of his skin to the features of his face, the sunken cheeks indicated malnutrition as a child. The steep forehead indicated hard surfaces at birth, and both factors indicated poverty. That was not a characteristic of a commander in most Roman legions—especially not one that wore the insignia he was wearing.

The old man was right. Bishkar was an Ostrogoth orphan that Attila had taken under his wing. Even though his Latin was strong, his accent had been corrupted with years of tribal dialects. If loyalty to Uther's father was not enough to keep his silence, the irritation at the man pretending to Roman sealed the deal.

Bouncing between acquiescence and reticence, the old man finally decided that he would not give in. Come what may, he decided, he would not reveal all he knew. But in addition to all of his qualities, Bishkar could read men with high accuracy. The old man had made a mistake of considering his next move—it was a signal to Bishkar that there was something to consider, and that, therefore, there was something to hide.

The only thing to hide now was the location of Uther and Arthur and that became his only objective for the moment. All other thoughts fell away from the young man who could turn his focus down to the last detail in his head and not back out of it.

Bishkar glared into the man's eyes, intent on extracting the information that lay behind them. Unsheathing his gladius, he presented the tip to the old man's throat and pushed it gently, signaling the old man to move back. The old man, petrified at first—a normal response—quickly steeled his resolve and prayed to his god for a swift death.

With the old man at the kitchen table, Bishkar reached for the washbasin and the kettle over the fire. He poured the water in and instructed the old man to place his shriveled hand into the scalding water. The old man found too much pride in him to resist but the reflex of pain and the fear of mutilation overrode his will. Eventually, Bishkar forced his hand in and let the old man squirm in pain as the boiling water scalded his hand and wrist.

The excruciating pain was not enough to unlock the secret from his chest, and this angered the general. He yanked the hand out of the water, pruned and scalded, then took his gladius and began peeling the skin of the old man's hands, all the while prompting him to reveal the location of the Uther and his son.

The old man died without a single revelation but not before spitting on the fake Roman.

Bishkar commanded his men to sack the farm and to take all they wanted but to leave the gold for him. As they ransacked the house, then the barn, they tripped on the passage that led to the underground vault.

It was clear to Bishkar who came to inspect it that it had been used recently. The wine and valuables that lay in the three chambers and the passageways was a large haul for the men and worth every minute they had spent traversing the peninsula.

Footprints on the floor, scrapes on the wall, told the sharp-minded Bishkar that something lay behind the rack on the southern wall. After an hour of trying, the door swung open to reveal another passage, now dark. Introducing the torch to the passage, he followed it till it reached the room where the occupants had already left. He couldn't figure how long, but it had to be no more than three days.

He was close, and more importantly, he had found their trail. But, unfortunately, he was too late.

16

VALLEY OF DEATH

VIPSANIUS HAD A PLAN TO fall back on. If they were to push the city into chaos, then the plan to rendezvous with Arthur would be at a location only known to him. He knew that Arthur, if successful, would ride with Uther to that location and they would meet later. His job was to keep that location a secret and just lead his men in a series of routes that would ferret out anyone who betrayed the company.

Once they had razed the south of the capital and rebellion had now reached critical mass, the signal to have his men leave the city was given. Each company knew where it had to go. They could not travel the roads out of Rome as one legion. Doing so would get them killed.

To tip things in their favor, they jettisoned their armor and swords and donned old tunics that covered whatever tattoos they may have had.

Before Lucius came to know of the uprising and that Uther had been liberated, Vipsanius and his men had filtered through the city, moving north, then exiting on different roads, some traveling alone, some in pairs, but never in groups more than three. Everyone had predetermined locations to meet. Once they were there, the next location would be given to them.

On the following black moon, Vipsanius was happy to see that three diversions later there had been no surprise attacks from the emperor's men. It assured him that none of his men had leaked the information and it was time to redirect the legion to the final rendezvous, a day's ride away. The soldiers were now reunited with their families. Ten thousand men now had swelled to twenty-five thousand men, women, and children.

As they lay amidst the trees of their homeland, each man dreamt of reuniting with their leader and of a day when the war would end, or a day when Rome would stop hounding them. It would come one day, but that was not on the horizon yet. But still, for now, for however brief, they felt a sense of peace descend in the silence of the valley. Pisae lay on the horizon, a mere league in distance. With a few tired lookouts perched on the perimeter, the rest fell asleep.

***

Horses neighed on the outskirts of the camp as fires burned to shield shivering soldiers from the blistering cold. As the heavens scattered snow, Attila and his lieutenants huddled in the main tent, where the old man's barn once stood. Having struck the alliance he needed with the emperor, he and the five thousand men in his charge rendezvoused at the old man's farm.

"We are fifty leagues from Rome, low on provisions and in range of a small town. The garrison there should be like any other. No more than five hundred men. We number ten thousand," Attila bellowed, hungry for another sacking.

"Reports have come in, sire," Bishkar said, "of Uther's legion a few leagues east of here. We could vanquish them now. After we sack the town, we march to engage them! They will be the first legion we defeat since the beginning of this campaign."

"They are well-trained. It will not be an easy fight," another one of Attila's commanders said.

"We've done it before," Albern, one of Attila's lieutenants, said. Attila didn't bother with his comment. He was nobody to the king of the barbarians.

"With the entire Hun army at our back," Rolstein added. The lieutenant in the rear guard was not as confident as some of the others in the tent. He felt the attack would be foolish. It didn't take long for the entire tent to erupt in dispute as the men shouted in typical Hun fashion.

"Enough!" Attila shouted, banging on the table with his fist, cracking the wood along its grain.

The room fell to silence.

"We are strong! We are the Huns!" he boomed. "We have fought the Empire for longer than any of us here can remember. We can beat them even if we are outnumbered. For it to be an even fight, every Hun has to be faced with five of those puny Romans."

The men roared at this imagery.

"They may have won with those odds before, but our fierceness has grown. Our skill and our drive are stronger than their puny swords. At dawn, we forget the town and we finish the Romans in the valley. We will defeat them, and send a rider back to Rome. He will tell Lucius of our victory, and the emperor will tremble at the thought of our existence. Any resistance or doubt will be met with punishment," he continued, to more cheers.

Hours later, dawn saw the Hun army assemble on the plains west of Pisae. The rains of the night had mustered a morning fog that swirled around the barbarian army as they stood there, brandishing their captured Roman weapons and their battle-axes.

Attila's commanders had already prepared the men—ten thousand hungry Huns awaited their prize. Attila rode out on his horse to the front of his army.

Donning his helmet, he spurred his horse into a run and led his army across the muddy plains, the black banner of his tribe streaming in the wind. Behind him, the men shouted as they charged. Thundering over the ridge as their feet pounded the ground, the sound served as an advance warning to the tired Romans still in slumber.

As they swooped down past the lookouts hanging from the trees with arrows in their necks, the horde rushed the center of the crowd, plowing through men, women, and children unprepared for war.

Attila brought his horse to a stop. As it neighed, rearing as it came to a stop, his men came to a halt behind him.

"Prepare for battle, men!" he shouted, and rode into a gallop again, leading his soldiers towards center mass as they shouted.

Within minutes, men in Attila's army began hurling javelins at the soldiers, and they landed accurately into the unprepared Romans. Chests, necks, and limbs were blown open by the javelins raining from behind the trees. By the time they saw a javelin, it was too late to move.

Attila drew his sword and shrieked with glee, an emotion that he always had before the thick of battle. Once the javelins ended, arrows began to rain down instead. Smaller, but with lethal accuracy, they took out soldier after soldier, many of whom hadn't even had the opportunity to find their weapon.

Chaos erupted as Attila's men surrounded the Romans, but were cut down in droves as they attempted to scatter the legions.

Rank after rank of Hun soldiers fell on the swords of the Romans who had taken a while to get focused, but once they did, they were as lethal as the attackers. Blood of Huns mingled with Romans' as each Hun took down three Romans, and each Roman only managed one Hun.

Bishkar slashed whatever came up beside him, banging on the shield of one Imperial soldier until he moved his shield and pushed his sword up to him. He dodged the blow and swung his sword to take the soldier's head off. As the Roman collapsed on the ground, he turned to engage the next soldier, his face mad and a loud growl emanating from his throat.

Many were not as lucky as him since most of them no longer had weapons, and they were forced into hand combat.

By the time it was all over, only a thousand Romans remained as they fled on foot.

***

By the next black moon, Arthur and Uther, and the thousand men who fled the valley with Vipsanius rendezvoused at the predetermined point just north of Mediolanum. The men who had arrived earlier had already set up camp. The ground was frozen mud. The air around them was bitter cold. With just a fraction of the men they once had, their fates were sealed. Whatever hopes they may have harbored to take back Rome, was now gone. Uther embraced his loyal commander.

"Vipsanius, you have done well, my old friend, under the circumstances. I am sorry for your loss."

"My lord, it is I who am sorry. We were tired and

MERLIN'S TOMB

did not choose the best place to camp. The Hun army attacked at dawn and we had no chance. Most of us had no weapons, many of us had families. We lost over twenty-four thousand men, women, and children."

The pain of the news showed on Uther's countenance. In contrast, Arthur's face showed anger.

Arthur pulled his father to the side, beyond earshot of the rest of the men.

"Father, I am afraid we have to leave tonight. Right away in fact. The only good thing about moving a thousand men is that we have horses for almost all of them, and we can move swiftly. The Huns cannot be far. We cannot allow them to close in on us as they now have a significant advantage."

"How many soldiers do we have?" Uther asked as he pondered Arthur's observation.

"In total, seven hundred soldiers, two hundred and thirty women, and seventy-eight children."

"I see no flaw in your assessment. I think it is wise we depart this night. See to it that the women and children ride in the center and men shield them in the front and rear."

Arthur relayed the order to Vipsanius who was exhausted but believed it to be the best course of action to begin the journey.

"Where are we going, my lord?"

"My old friend, I don't think even father knows that. For now, we will head to Aquitania. We can't go north as the Ostrogoths have allied with the Huns. We can't go west as the tribes there have allied with Lucius. Our only option is to thread the needle and head northwest. From here onward, we carry no more Roman titles and insignia. My father and I are merely Uther and Arthur."

"I understand. My… my apologies. It will take some getting used to. We will be ready in under an hour, Arthur."

17

VANISHED

"WHERE ARE THEY? IT HAS been a month and we are still tooling around the Italian peninsula," Attila barked.

Bishkar stood silent. His king was upset with him, but no more upset than he was with himself. How did they vanish? The Huns had searched the remains of the Romans in the valley but had not found any sign of Uther and Arthur. The men were happy with the loot they had amassed in the last week, but the objective had not been met and now they were down to five thousand men.

"Sire, we have to head north."

"Yet, by my calculation, Rome is in the south," Attila shot back.

"Well, yes. But it depends on what your priorities are. Do you want the seat of the palace, or do you want Uther's head on a platter?"

"I want it both and I want his son drawn and quartered."

"Which do you want first?"

Attila turned silent. He had watched how Bishkar had conducted himself this far. All their gains were because of him and he had performed better than Adolphus could have. Attila knew what Bishkar was asking him. And he had done it without any malice. In fact, he was doing it as an ally.

"My priority is to vanquish Rome."

"Well then, the answer is clear."

"How so?"

"If you want to vanquish Rome, then you have to go after Uther. If you want to vanquish Uther, you have to kill Lucius."

Attila, for the first time in his life, stood bewildered. He did not understand the logic of the strategy, and Bishkar could see that.

"So where do we go since we do not know where Uther is going?"

"I can guess that he is going to Paris. That would be one of two options. He has to go as far away from Rome as he can and Rome's influence with the Franks is diminishing. That is the only safe harbor he will have."

"We can't travel on Visigoth land."

"But we can travel on Ostrogoth land and that will

take us all the way to Divodurum, and from there, we can head west to Paris. And, along the way, we can bulk up our expendables. We have none now, and the expendables can make up the largest part of our defenses. Those who survive after three battles can be inducted into another division. That division will be able to share in the booty. It will give them something to live for."

"The men are not going to like it."

"Leave that to me, sire."

Attila nodded. "So we sack every town between here and Paris?"

"Not every town, only the towns on the Visigoth land. We can also recruit more men among the tribes in the east. I believe by the time we get to Paris, you should be thirty-thousand men strong."

"Make it happen. When will we leave?"

"We can leave in three days. We have much to prepare for, and we have plenty of loot to organize. Three days will give us enough time to do all that."

"So be it."

***

"Titus, where are Attila and his men?" Lucius had grown grim. Events beyond the palace where he sat fat, were not moving at the pace he had hoped.

"They are still outside Pisae, sire."

"Why hasn't he apprehended Uther?"

"Reports indicate that the Huns have all but decimated the two legions along with their families."

"All of them?"

"Pretty much, sire."

"Are you telling me that Uther no longer has an army?"

"Yes, sire. He is but one man."

"Charge him in absentia for treason, and his son as well. His family name is to be stripped from the rolls, and all his properties are to be confiscated right away."

"Yes, sire. Right away."

"Send a legion to track Attila from a distance. I want reports daily on where they are and where they are going. I don't trust that primate."

"Good idea, sire."

A month passed and the daily reports that arrived told of a sedate and boring series of events. The Huns had continued to sack and raid towns on the western side of their northward trek while continually increasing their men from eastern tribes. All the while, an entire legion of the Roman army tread north, extending the supply lines that came from Mediolanum. It was becoming an expensive proposition during a time when Rome's taxes were no longer enough to support its status and the emperor's lifestyle.

18

THE ENCHANTED FOREST

THE LAST LEG OF THE journey north had been long. The depths of winter and the high latitudes magnified each minute on a horse's back to make it seem like an hour. The journey had been uneventful and the two Pendragon men grew more anxious as each step brought them closer to the moment they would see Igraine.

As each step advanced toward the Forest of Broceliande, they seemed to leave behind the shade of their Roman selves, continuously practicing the tongue of their adopted land. Encounters with the Franks this far north had made them better in the tongue than they had thought they might have been. But learning a new language for father and son was not a hard thing. Both were already well-versed in Latin and Greek.

"Why did you and Mother choose this place?" Arthur asked as they traveled the last leg of the journey. The Forest now lay just ahead, over the horizon.

Uther realized that it was time for him to tell his son some things about his mother that he had not known. But not all of it.

"Your mother has a connection to this forest," Uther began, as Arthur tried to suppress his bewilderment that his mother would have anything to do with a forest that was the center of folklore.

"She tried to tell me that all things have more meaning to it than what our senses can detect. She believes the mind is a sort of sense too. As your eyes see things, your mind can think of things as well."

"I don't understand, Father. Of course, my eyes see and my mind can think."

Uther smiled, knowing very well that he was not the one to explain these things to his son. His wife was better at it. But still, he had to light the spark in his own mind so that the questions could flow, and Igraine could help answer them later.

"Think of it this way. If you see an object, you do so with your eyes. You can't see it with your ears or with your nose. Yes?"

"Yes," Arthur answered, not sure where his father was going with this.

"In the same way, your mind can perceive things. Your thoughts do not happen in a vacuum, they happen because it exists in reality. Just think about that until you have a chance to talk to your mother about it."

Arthur kept silent, suddenly feeling that there was truth to what his father was trying to tell him, but he was not fully grasping it.

"What does that have to do with coming here?"

"Open your mind, and see what it has to offer. What comes next will become apparent to you at that point."

"Do you not know what comes next, Father?"

"No, Arthur. All my life has been about Rome. The first part of my life was about becoming a man who would protect Rome, following in my father's footsteps. The second part of my life was about building armies so that Rome could expand and that we could bring civilization to the weak-minded and the backward. Then it was about protecting Rome. It has always been about Rome. Now, Rome is somewhere back there. Too far away for my feet to walk and too far for my mind to think."

"And, now without Rome, you have no purpose. Is that what you think?"

"Yes. I am here for the same reason you are—to find direction."

"And how will that forest provide us with that direction?"

"Like I said, I don't know. But this was your mother's idea, and I have learned never to question it."

Arthur understood exactly what his father meant.

The rest of the journey passed as slowly as it did silently, each man in his own thought. They arrived at the edge of the forest as the winter sun submerged in the southwestern sky and a full moon hung among the stars. A cloudless night contributed to the cold that pierced their cloaks and numbed their faces. Horses blew vapor from their nostrils like dragons breathing fire as they carried their burden. The edge of the forest was a silent scene, made darker by the thick canopy of branches, bare of leaves since the autumn. In its wake, the departure of green left the wrangled twisting branches curled like the knobbly fingers of an old witch attempting to cast a spell.

It was a ghostly experience, and Arthur's discomfort was shared by everyone in the train of travelers, including the horses. Uther could sense the discomfort that resided in everyone there. He was the only one who didn't give their predicament or their location a second thought. His feelings were dominated by the hope that he would soon be reunited with his wife.

The path grew difficult to navigate as whatever remaining ambient light vanished, robbed by a cloud of fog that hung over the forest.

"It's time to set up camp, Father."

"I think that's best," Uther replied, answering with trepidation as his heart wished they could go on and find his wife who he was certain was not far.

Arthur instructed Vipsanius to set up camp, then,

leaving his horse with one of the other soldiers, threw his cloak around his head for added warmth and proceeded into the forest. On foot and all alone, Arthur moved. His gait was strong, unrepresentative of the fatigue that stretched across his bones. The attraction to enter the forest was overwhelming, but reason was scarce. He knew what he had to do but didn't know why he had to do it.

As he advanced, the sounds of his people dismounting and setting up camp gradually faded away and the sound of the forest's night began to merge with his consciousness. Critters, hidden from sight, echoed their concern of an intruder as Arthur continued to make his way, able to only see a few feet in front of him.

Long after the sounds of his people faded in the rear and the cacophony of the critters faded into the darkness, Arthur happened upon a clearing. Above him, the speckle of starlight was enough to illuminate the land beneath his feet. The eerie silence piqued his senses as he tried to listen beyond the natural edge of his hearing, but for the first time in his life, only absolute silence engulfed him and he could hear the sound of his thoughts with such clarity that memories and imagination melted into one.

In front of him, his eyes now picked up a granite slab. At first, it looked like an altar of some kind, but as he moved closer, its shape and angle suggested something different. His curiosity compelled further investigation as he moved over slowly, periodically checking his surroundings for anyone that might have been hiding in the shadows. He was alone.

The granite structure stood waist-high and was as broad as Arthur's outstretched arms and as long as the height he occupied from head to toe. It occurred to him that it was a tomb.

"Why would there be a tomb in the middle of the forest?" he whispered.

"It is the tomb of Merlin the Mage," a voice boomed, causing Arthur to snap around and survey his surroundings.

Once again, he found no one there. Only silence and emptiness.

Arthur tried to refocus. The hair on the nape of his neck was now standing at full alert as shivers bounced along his spine. His eyes found it hard to focus. Between the ringing in his head and the lack of light to distinguish his depth of field, Arthur grew confused.

Not daring to utter another whisper, he posed his next question within the space of his own mind.

Who is Merlin?

No answer came forth. Only silence dominated the scene as Arthur struggled to comprehend his find. The confluence of events robbed him of his confidence to act as he stood frozen harboring only one desire—to touch the marble tomb of Merlin the Mage.

With no other source of thought to guide him, Arthur followed his desires and reached for the marble slab and touched it, only to trigger a blinding flash that threw him

MERLIN'S TOMB

from his stance and knocked him off his feet. All at once the dark forest transformed into a meadow, undulating from the apex where he stood toward a lush green forest below and a bay below that encircled an ocean darker than the blue of the Mediterranean.

"You are not safe here, child of Pendragon," a nebulous voice echoed.

"What harm could come to me here, on this hill, atop this forest, over this sea?"

"Here no harm will come to you, but this is only where your mind is and your mind cannot stay apart from your body for long. It has to return to where your body is, and that place presents an imminent danger."

"Who is telling me this?"

"My name is Merlin."

"You are Merlin the Mage?"

"I shall not be so arrogant as to call myself a mage. But what they call me after I die, I cannot control."

"Are you the spirit of Merlin?"

"No. I am Merlin and I am not far from where you are now. Just beyond the Germanicus Ocean, above the Narrow Sea."

"You are in Britannia?"

"Yes," the voice said.

It occurred to Arthur that he had to test this voice. It seemed to suggest that it knew all things, but how could Arthur be sure unless he tested it?

"Where is my mother?" he asked, trying to keep incredulity beneath the surface.

"Your mother is right next to you."

Arthur turned to look around him, but all he saw was green pastures and bright skies. Before he could register his disagreement with the answer, the voice spoke once more.

"Sail up the Narrows until you come to the neck of Britannia in the north. You will see an inlet. Sail into that."

"Why should I trust you?"

The voice scoffed. "Search your thoughts. You will know if my intentions are honorable or malicious."

"Are you speaking to me from beyond?"

The voice chuckled. "I am speaking from beyond the ocean."

"That's not what I mean."

"I know what you mean, and I have answered you. Do not give in to what your eyes see, but balance it with what your heart knows."

And with that, the bright light, along with the meadow, forest, and ocean vanished and Arthur was thrown back into the all-penetrating darkness of the Forest of Broceliande. Only this time, there was something with him in the darkness.

As his mind cleared and his eyes reaccustomed to the darkness, he found Igraine by his side, kneeling to tend to her son.

"Mother?" he whispered.

"It is good to see you, my child. We have waited far too long for your arrival."

"I am happy to see you as well, Mother. Have you seen Father?"

"Not yet. They are in the midst of setting up camp."

"What is this tomb, Mother?"

"It is where the prophecies dictate that the one called Merlin will be laid to rest once his time here comes to an end."

"You know him?"

"I know of him. He is the child of the prophecy that my people have spoken about for ages. He will come into power later, but for now, you should make him an ally."

"In that case, we have to hurry," he said, rising to embrace his mother.

The two ran through the forest, eventually finding Uther and the others in the midst of their labor. Uther broke down in tears at the sight of his wife. It was a sight that Arthur had never seen, but it confirmed the depth of love he knew his father had for his mother.

"Vipsanius," Arthur called. "We cannot stay here. It is time to go."

"But we just got here. The people are tired, Arthur," he replied, already getting used to addressing Arthur by name.

"I understand your concern, my old friend, but the danger is imminent."

Vipsanius looked to Uther for clarity. Uther was

equally perplexed. The people were indeed tired and there was no sign of any danger. But Igraine interceded. "Arthur is right. The danger is imminent, and we need to move."

Uther detected truth in both their voices and nodded to Vipsanius who snapped out of his disbelief and put his full heart into it.

"Where are we going?" Vipsanius asked as he set to prepare the caravan.

"I don't know yet, but it would have to be north."

"The forest gets thicker in the north, Arthur. What is your eventual destination?"

Uther looked at his son.

"To the coast," Arthur finally revealed.

"And then?"

"And then to Britannia," Arthur answered Vipsanius.

"What?" Vipsanius jumped. "You want to cross the Narrows?"

Arthur did not respond but passed him a look that was clear in its message that time was being wasted while they talked. Vipsanius got the message and proceeded to make the necessary preparations.

With his loyal lieutenant gone, Arthur turned to his parents. "We are in danger if we stay here and we have to go. I can't explain to you how I know, but trust me, Father."

"Of course, my son, I trust you." And with that, the weary, deciding to not burden their horses, walked the rest of the way, heading toward Paris. There, they believed they would be able to find the ships they needed to transport them up to their destination.

C.J. BROWN

19

VOYAGE

"WE WILL CAMP HERE TONIGHT, sire," Bishkar said as he rode up to his king. The road had been long and the troops had been marching for more than twenty hours.

The king gave his assent. Now at the head of almost thirty-thousand men, his goal was to take control of Paris. With Paris under his thumb, he was certain he would be able to capture Uther and bring his revenge to fruition, and find peace within his heart once more.

It wasn't until past midnight that the Hun army, the expendables, and the new company of men, began the process of setting up camp. In the last month, they had restocked and resupplied their numbers and were now stronger than they had hoped to be—and significantly richer after sacking town after town in a trail of destruction that stretched out behind them from Genua to Paris. Bishkar had outperformed Attila's expectation in rebuilding the army.

On the night of the black moon, the men stretched out over the horizon and the people within the city of Paris could see the eastern horizon fill with flickers of campfires. The Frankish king was alerted to the possibility of an invasion and a small troop of reconnaissance soldiers was dispatched to spy on them.

When King Merovech was advised by his spies just before dawn that it was Attila the Hun who sat on the horizon, the king immediately sounded the horns for the army and the populace to rise in defense of the city. The call to arms was heeded to by young and old, short and tall across the Sequana River that flowed through Paris.

By dawn, the Huns had reanimated their ranks and the obnoxious battle drums and cries of the Hun army could be heard on the horizon.

"They are here," Arthur declared, as they arrived at the port, ready to board the ships that would sail them across the Narrow Sea.

Vipsanius could now see the wisdom of Arthur's decision to move the night before and not be complacent. As the city of Paris went to war with the hordes that attacked from the western horizon, Arthur and his

MERLIN'S TOMB

people had boarded the trade vessels that were headed to Caledonii.

As they sailed up the Sequena River and made it to the estuary, they could see the city, now in flames and Uther bowed his head wondering if he was to blame for the sacking of the city. If it weren't for his presence here, the Hun army would not have ventured this far north.

"Who are they?" Arthur asked the vessel's captain, pretending to not know that it was the Huns.

"Barbarians, my lord. They are here to sack my city."

"Have they come before?"

"No. Never like this while the Romans protected us. But now Rome is weak. The true emperor is no longer on the throne that is occupied by a coward," the captain answered, seeming to understand the politics of a land far away.

"Will they be able to vanquish your city?"

"No, my lord. The Franks have been building a defense system that the world does not know about. They will see it for the first time today. The Romans no longer protect us, but we will protect ourselves and the Huns will fall before nightfall."

Arthur smiled, for the first time seeing the sight of a stranger that was as honorable as the Romans of the old days. It had been a long time since he saw this much love for one's land and this much honor within the chest of one man. Rome had long lost that, and that, among other reasons, was why Arthur could no longer remain loyal to the empire, or count himself as a citizen.

As the vessel passed the estuary and headed out to sea, Arthur turned his back on the continent and looked forward to the open waters. Having never set his eyes on the Narrows Sea or Britannia, a world of opportunity awaited him and the small band of people he led.

Behind the last ship in Arthur's convoy, another ship set sail. This one carried a full crew but only one passenger— Bishkar. His orders to the merchant ship captain were to trail the convoy in front and go wherever it went but to stay just over the horizon from it. Bishkar's goal was to follow the last of the noble Romans. Even if it meant going to the ends of the earth and hunting him down.

NEWSLETTER

This is the first book in the Pendragon Legend. If you enjoyed Book 1, don't miss out on following releases by signing up for my newsletter. Make sure to sign up at the link below!

[NEWSLETTER SIGNUP FORM](#)

ABOUT THE AUTHOR

C.J. Brown has a lifelong passion for fantasy books and she quit her career in marketing to pursue her dream of becoming an author. Legends and myths in particular strike her fancy, and she loves putting her own spin on them. An adventurer at heart, when not writing, she can be found exploring the old mystical Northwoods around her home, where she finds much of her inspiration.

Website: cj-brown.com

Facebook: fb.me/cjbrown78

Thanks for reading. Please consider leaving a review—it means a lot!

Printed in Poland
by Amazon Fulfillment
Poland Sp. z o.o., Wrocław
03 November 2022

2f45904e-8947-490a-ab2c-2cc9d67612abR01